The Ghost Wind Stallion

A Kaya Mystery

by Emma Carlson Berne

★ American Girl®

Published by American Girl Publishing
Copyright © 2016 American Girl

Questions or comments? Call 1-800-845-0005, visit **americangirl.com,** or write
to Customer Service, American Girl, 8400 Fairway Place, Middleton, WI 53562.

Printed in China
16 17 18 19 20 21 LEO 11 10 9 8 7 6 5 4 3 2 1

All American Girl marks, BeForever™, and Kaya™
are trademarks of American Girl.

This book is a work of fiction. Any similarity to real persons, living or dead,
is coincidental and not intended by American Girl. References to real events,
people, or places are used fictitiously. Other names, characters, places, and
incidents are the products of imagination.

Special thanks to Ann McCormack,
Cultural Arts Coordinator for the Nez Perce Tribe

Cover image by Juliana Kolesova

The following individuals and organizations have given permission to use
images incorporated into the cover design: image of horses, bottom panel,
© iStock.com/Zuzule; elements of border pattern, © iStock.com/Bassarida;
meadow background, upper panel, © iStock.com/Thundor; background
pattern on back cover, © kristypargeter/Crestock.

Cataloging-in-Publication Data available from the Library of Congress

americangirl.com/service

For Jess—
my "sister" for the last thirty years

Beforever™

The adventurous characters you'll meet in
the BeForever books will spark your curiosity
about the past, inspire you to find your voice
in the present, and excite you about your future.
You'll make friends with these girls as you share
their fun and their challenges. Like you, they are
bright and brave, imaginative and energetic,
creative and kind. Just as you are, they are
discovering what really matters: Helping others.
Being a true friend. Protecting the earth.
Standing up for what's right. Read their stories,
explore their worlds, join their adventures.
Your friendship with them will BeForever.

TABLE *of* CONTENTS

Kaya and her family are Nimíipuu,
known today as Nez Perce Indians.
They speak the Nez Perce language,
so you'll see some Nez Perce words
in this book. "Kaya" is short for the
Nez Perce name Kaya'aton'my',
which means "she who arranges rocks."
You'll find the meanings and pronunciations
of these and other Nez Perce words
in the glossary on page 208.

chapter 1
A Sister's Wish

KAYA CROUCHED LOW over Steps High's neck, her legs clinging to the mare's slick black sides. She felt her horse's muscles bunch and release, bunch and release beneath her while the heavy hooves of competing horses beat a rhythm in the dirt at either side. Her pulse beat the same rhythm in her ears as the wind whipped her face and sweaty hair.

To her right, the boy called Raven shouted to urge his chestnut forward. The horse sprang ahead, but Kaya steered Steps High slightly closer to him. The chestnut slackened his speed, feeling crowded by Steps High. "Good girl!" Kaya shouted and pressed her heels more firmly to her mare's ribs. She pushed the reins up on Steps High's neck and the mare surged ahead.

1

Now four horses were behind them, but the flashing hooves of a white-spotted mare pounded the earth
in front of them. Her rider, Rabbit—a girl a little older
than Kaya—threw a glance over her shoulder at Steps
High, her eyes wide.

"We can do it, girl!" Kaya muttered, clenching
her teeth.

From the corner of her eye, Kaya glimpsed the
crowd of children on the sidelines, jumping up and
down in the long grass of the Weippe Prairie as they
cheered the racers on. In the distance, the camas mead-
ows were blanketed with the withered brown tops of
the harvested plants. Kaya, her sister Speaking Rain,
and the rest of their family had come with their band
to dig camas roots on the Weippe Prairie with many
other bands of *Nimíipuu*. Now, in the late summer, the
time of digging was almost finished. Soon they would
travel a little higher into the mountains to pick berries.
But for now, out here on the flat racing ground, the
world was all dirt and sweat and excitement—and

the race was a welcome break from the hard work of digging roots.

"Come on!" Kaya shouted. She felt Steps High flatten out, stretching her nose. The white-spotted rump grew closer and closer. Carefully, inch by inch, Kaya maneuvered Steps High until they were running neck and neck with Rabbit. Then she steered Steps High ever so slightly to the left, guiding her so close to Rabbit's mare that the horses' legs almost touched. It was a trick Kaya's father, *Toe-ta,* had taught her to throw the other horse off its speed. Kaya's stomach flipped as her horse almost bumped Rabbit's. If there was contact, she'd be disqualified and possibly trip the other horse. She seemed to hear her father's voice in her head. *Use your skill as a horsewoman wisely. Be bold, be brave, but do not be foolish.* Quickly, she turned Steps High's nose slightly to the right. The finish line, marked by two rocks, loomed ahead.

"Go, Kaya!" she faintly heard someone shout. It sounded like her sister Speaking Rain. Speaking Rain was blind, but Kaya knew that another girl would be standing with her on the sidelines, describing every detail of the race.

Her heart surged at her sister's voice. Even Steps High seemed to respond. Kaya could feel her mare gather her strength. Rabbit's horse pounded alongside, but she was flagging, Kaya could see. She fell back. Steps High pulled ahead. The finish line flashed past them, and Kaya knew they had won.

"We did it, girl!" Kaya murmured to her horse as she circled Steps High in a wide arc, slowing her to a rapid trot and then a fast walk. Triumph filled her, and she wanted to shriek aloud. But of course she would never gloat at a victory in that way. Kaya's people, the Nimíipuu, always tried to be humble and not brag.

"Nice riding," Rabbit said, trotting up to her. Sweat glistened on her round face, and her braids were disheveled. Kaya was sure her own were just as windblown.

"*Katsee-yow-yow,*" Kaya thanked her modestly.

"We were very close there at the end. You ran a good race."

Rabbit gave her a friendly smile and rode off to where the children were organizing another race.

Patting Steps High's neck, hot and wet with foamy sweat, Kaya thought back to the very first race she'd run, three years ago. She'd pushed Steps High to race before the mare was properly trained, just to prove to her cousins Fox Tail and Raven that her horse was the fastest. And she'd paid for her boasting dearly. Steps High had bucked, and Kaya had lost the race.

Kaya let out a deep breath as she slid off Steps High. Both she and her horse had grown up a lot since then.

Kaya led Steps High over to the sidelines. The other children had scattered, and now her sister stood alone. Speaking Rain, a slim girl with long braids and cloudy eyes, turned her head at the sound of Steps High's footsteps.

"Speaking Rain, I won!" Kaya said. It felt good to share this moment with her sister. Speaking Rain spent part of every year with another tribe, the *Salish*, who were friends of the Nimíipuu. There she lived with an old woman named White Braids, who had rescued her after she was captured by enemies. Speaking Rain loved White Braids as a second mother, but Kaya missed her sister during the months she spent away. She'd been delighted to welcome Speaking Rain home just a few sleeps before.

A smile spread over her sister's face. "I'm so glad for you!" Speaking Rain gave Kaya a little hug. "And Steps High, too. You have trained her well, Sister."

"I have trained her for a long time, that is true," Kaya said. "We should take Steps High back to the herd. Then we'd better get home and help *Eetsa* prepare for Tall Branch's arrival."

Their mother's sister, Tall Branch, was coming to live with the family. She had married into another band of Nimíipuu and had lived far away for many years—so many, in fact, that Kaya had never met her. Tall Branch's husband had recently died, and she had no children, so Tall Branch had decided to come live with Kaya's family. Her band did not move around according to the seasons as Kaya's band did, but instead lived year-round in a village on the river. They had just moved downriver and set up a new village only a half day's ride from the prairie where Kaya's band was living during the camas root harvest. Last night, a messenger had arrived to tell them that a party bringing Tall Branch was set to arrive around midday tomorrow.

The girls walked slowly toward the meadow where the horse herd was kept, with Steps High following on a loose rein. Speaking Rain held a pinch of Kaya's deerskin dress and walked a step behind her as she always had. Her sister's touch felt as familiar to Kaya as that of her own hand.

Kaya stopped Steps High near the vast horse herd that was spread out in a meadow a short distance from the camp. Dark pine trees on one side provided a background for the chestnut, gray, black, and white-spotted horses, about a hundred in all, that ranged out among the waving grasses, peacefully grazing in the sunshine, tails swishing.

"I'm so glad we raced well, my horse," Kaya said to Steps High as she slipped off her bridle. She pulled a deerskin cloth from her waist pouch and quickly gave the mare's legs a rubdown. Then she watched her horse amble away into the herd.

"*Aa-heh.* You and your horse are truly one, just as we Nimíipuu always hope that a horse and rider will be." Speaking Rain's words were warm, but her voice was low, as if she were holding something back. Kaya thought of a boulder wedged against the mouth of a stream.

Kaya turned. "What is wrong, my sister?" She looked into Speaking Rain's face. Underneath the smile, she could see a shadow as well.

"It's just that... ever since I returned from the Salish, I've been wishing..." Speaking Rain paused, her hands pleating a fold of her skirt.

"Wishing what?" Kaya asked.

Speaking Rain shook her head as they began walking toward the bustling tepee camp. "I'm not wise to even think of it."

"Tell me," Kaya urged her sister. Speaking Rain was silent for several minutes as they walked along the narrow path that led from the herd pasture, through part of the camas field, and then on to the camp. Kaya could see the conical reed-covered peaks of the tepees jutting up in a circle. She caught sight of their grandmother *Kautsa* standing outside their family's tepee, looking for them. Kaya stopped Speaking Rain on the path and looked into her sister's face that she knew so well.

"It's just that... Kaya, we're growing up." Speaking Rain looked almost desperate. "You and the others take good care of me. But I don't want to be taken care of. I want to do things on my own." She rubbed the pinch of Kaya's dress that she was holding. "I don't want to be led."

"But—" Kaya started to interrupt. She wanted to erase the longing in her sister's voice.

Speaking Rain held up her hand. "No, no—I mean, I *know* I have to be led sometimes. But . . . I've always wished I could ride alone, without you or someone else to guide me." She mumbled these last words as if she wished to swallow them. "When I'm with White Braids . . . well, she *needs* me to help her. She's old, and I can make things we need and rub her back at night when it aches. But here, you and our parents love me, but . . . you don't *need* me."

"But we do!" Kaya insisted. "We need you so much. You are my sister and my friend. You make the best rope and mats and baskets for us. You cook and help with our little brothers—" She broke off and grasped her sister's hands. "We do need you," she said, low.

Speaking Rain squeezed Kaya's hands back. "I know. It's just that I want to be more than someone who sits on a mat and weaves. I want to ride out with

you when we go into the mountains to pick berries—
by your side, not behind you. If I could do that, I could
really be your sister: equal. I could help our people, and
not be a burden."

The pain in her voice startled Kaya. "I didn't know
you felt that way," she said.

Speaking Rain sighed and shrugged. "Perhaps I'm
not wise to wish for things that can't possibly come
true. I'll be all right. Don't worry about me."

But I am worried, Kaya thought as they walked into
camp. She had always helped Speaking Rain before.
But how could she help her this time?

chapter 2
Nighttime Mystery

WHEN KAYA AND Speaking Rain arrived at the camp, everyone was bustling around preparing for Tall Branch's arrival. The girls plunged into the activity, too.

Kaya was busy for the rest of the day. She pulled the heavy sleeping rolls around inside the tepee to make a place for Tall Branch to sleep. She rearranged the neatly stacked bundles encased in hide that sat on the floor and the baskets that hung from the poles so that Tall Branch would have a spot to put her own things. She even swept the dirt floor of the tepee with pine boughs so that it would be especially fresh and clean. But when she got into her sleeping furs that night and snuggled up next to Speaking Rain, she lay awake for a long time, listening to the slow, peaceful breathing of her family all around her. Speaking Rain's words from earlier today swirled in her head. Kaya's heart twisted to think that her sister was troubled. But how could she help her? Kaya turned to one side and then the other until finally, somehow, she fell asleep.

Kaya woke with a start sometime later. She listened to her heart hammering in the dark of the tepee. All around her, the quiet night air was filled with slow night breathing. Kaya strained her ears. Was that a rustle just outside? She waited, but heard nothing more.

Slowly, Kaya eased back onto the soft furs of her sleeping roll and pulled the deerskin up to her nose. She sighed and turned over, wanting to snuggle close to Speaking Rain.

But Speaking Rain's place was empty.

Kaya sat up, her eyes wide. She groped in the furs. Speaking Rain's side of the bed was cold. Her sister was gone.

Moving as quietly as she could, Kaya reached for her folded deerskin dress by the side of the bed and pulled it on. Perhaps her sister had gone out to the latrine. *Why didn't she wake me?* Kaya thought. Her sister had never left the tepee alone at night before. Kaya flashed on their conversation after the race. Speaking Rain wanted to do things on her own. Had she gone off somewhere by herself?

Softly, Kaya crept from the tepee. A half-moon hung low in the sky, throwing a dim light on the tepees all around her. Shivering in the cool night air, Kaya scanned the camp for her sister, but everything was still and silent. At the edge of the camp, Kaya saw the dark silhouettes of a few tethered horses, their heads drooping in sleep. Farther away, she could just make out a dark smudge that was the rest of the horse herd. Beyond that, stretching in all directions in the darkness, was the endless Weippe Prairie.

Speaking Rain was out here somewhere. Kaya stood still, watching and listening.

Then a dark shape moved near the tethered horses. Kaya's muscles tensed. A wolf? Or a mountain lion?

The shape moved and straightened up. In the faint moonlight, Kaya could see that it was a person—a girl in a deerskin dress.

Kaya walked softly over to her. "Speaking Rain?" Kaya whispered. "Are you all right? What are you doing out here?"

But Speaking Rain didn't answer. She was making movements with her hands as if she were lifting something, smoothing something out—but her hands were empty.

"Speaking Rain?" Kaya said more loudly. Her sister didn't seem to hear her. She didn't even lift her head.

Kaya edged closer. What was wrong with her sister? Then she noticed that Speaking Rain's eyes were closed. She was sleepwalking.

Kaya paused, unsure what to do. Her sister had never sleepwalked before. And what was she doing with her hands? She was still making phantom movements in the air, performing some action that might make sense only in her dream. Yet something about her gestures seemed familiar. Kaya watched, trying to place what it was. Then her sister slowly raised both hands above her head as if she were lifting something broad and heavy, and seemed to place it carefully on something else. *She's saddling a horse!* Kaya realized in a flash. Except there was no saddle and no horse, just her sleeping sister and the empty night air.

Kaya watched as her sister cinched the imaginary saddle and slipped a bit into an invisible horse's mouth. Then she gave the imaginary horse a pat and turned and walked right past Kaya, so close that Kaya could hear her breath. She made her way through the camp to their tepee, opened the flap, and disappeared inside.

Moving as lightly as she could, Kaya hurried to follow her. By the time she slipped into the dark tepee, her sister was already back in their bed, asleep. Kaya eased into the furs beside her. But she lay awake a long time, gazing up at the bit of night sky visible above the tepee poles, listening to Speaking Rain's slow breathing beside her, unable to shake what she had seen. Why had her sister sleepwalked? Was her desire to ride alone so important that she had to act it out in a dream?

"It is morning! We are alive! The sun is witness to what we do today! Our new relative, Tall Branch, arrives today! We welcome her with joy to our family!"

Kaya opened her eyes to the sound of the crier who walked among the tepees, rousing people and calling out the events of the day. The door flap was pulled aside, and sunlight flooded the tepee. Beside her, Speaking Rain sat up too, her braids rumpled, and yawned.

Toe-ta was gone already, out to check the horse herd as he did every morning, and Eetsa sat with Kaya's young twin brothers, Wing Feather and Sparrow, combing out their hair. Kautsa smiled at Kaya and Speaking Rain, her deep wrinkles crinkling her cheeks. "We must hurry this morning, girls. We must finish making ready for Tall Branch. Here are some finger cakes for your breakfast. Take them with you and run down to the river to bathe." She handed them the little finger-sized cakes made from ground kouse root.

Outside the tepee, the morning air sparkled with freshness. Dew glistened on the prairie grasses, brown and green with the end of the summer. Speaking Rain and Kaya hurried along the path that led to the river, where they bathed in the cold water each morning. Speaking Rain held a pinch of Kaya's dress, as usual. But this morning, Kaya had heard her sister heave a deep sigh as she took hold of the little piece of fringe.

"*Tawts may-we*, Daughters," Toe-ta greeted them. Kaya's father, a powerful man with a deep voice, was leading a large brown-and-white horse by a rope. "You must bathe, so you can greet our visitors. I'll join you back at camp as soon as I clean this horse's hooves. He picked up some sharp gravel in his feet last night."

"Aa-heh, we'll be ready to greet our aunt," Speaking Rain assured Toe-ta.

"Do you remember what happened last night?"

Kaya asked quietly, as they trotted down the sloping
path to the riverbank.

"No, what happened?" her sister asked.

"You were sleepwalking," Kaya said. She recounted
what she'd seen in the night. "And it looked as if in your
dream you were getting a horse ready to ride. Do you
remember your dream?"

A cloud passed over Speaking Rain's cheerful face.
"I do now," she said. Her voice was low. "But come, it's
time to bathe. We'll talk while we wash."

Soon, they reached the river. Girls were already
splashing in the cold mountain water as grandmothers
supervised on the riverbank. Kaya and Speaking Rain
slipped out of their dresses and waded into the icy-
clear water.

Kaya dunked her head and splashed some water
at Rabbit, who grinned back. Then she led Speaking
Rain a short distance downstream, out of earshot of the
other girls. "Now," she said, eyeing her sister. "Tell me
your dream."

Speaking Rain looked as if she wished Kaya hadn't remembered to ask. She swam slowly in a small circle, her cloudy eyes gazing into the distance but seeing nothing. "I dreamed I was riding a beautiful horse. He galloped as lightly as a breeze touches your cheek." Her voice was soft, as if she were telling her story to herself. "His coat was as soft to the hand as a rabbit's fur. And I rode on his back alone. It was just the two of us. We had no guide, and no rope led us. We galloped across the prairie as if we were one being." Her voice trailed off and she was quiet.

"Your dream is powerful," Kaya said respectfully.

Speaking Rain seemed to break out of her reverie. "I don't know about this dream." She began to swim briskly for the bank, using the sound of the grand-mothers' voices to guide her. Kaya followed.

Climbing out of the water, they rubbed themselves with the deerskins a grandmother handed them and pulled their dresses on. "It's just wishing. That's all— like I told you yesterday. I'm sure Kautsa is waiting for us." Speaking Rain's voice was back to normal.

They walked swiftly back toward the camp. Kaya wanted to ask more questions, but her sister had said she didn't want to think about the dream further. Kaya had to honor Speaking Rain's wish. Anyway, they had to get ready for Tall Branch's arrival.

"There you are, Granddaughters!" Kautsa called when she saw them. Eetsa sat beside her on a mat, weaving a basket. "I thought the Stick People had carried you away." She smiled to soften her words. The Stick People were wily beings who lived in the deep woods. They could leave signs to help people who were lost or send warnings of danger. But they could also carry away food, or even a child, especially if they thought they were being disrespected. "We must prepare some refreshment for Tall Branch. She will be hungry and thirsty after her journey."

"Aa-heh, we will," Kaya said, excitement rising in her. It would be different, having a whole new member of the family. Not like when the band had visitors.

Tall Branch would be here for good. "I thought I would prepare rose-hip tea to serve to our aunt when she arrives. Everyone likes that."

"That is the Nimíipuu way." Kautsa smiled at them. "We'll make her feel welcome in her new home."

"Be sure to make the tea just right." Eetsa looked up from her weaving. "I remember that Tall Branch likes her tea very strong. You will know if it is not to her liking." A little frown creased her forehead and Kaya heard her mother sigh.

"Of course we will," Kaya reassured her mother. She didn't know why Eetsa looked troubled.

Kaya placed a few smooth stones into the cooking fire and filled a tightly woven basket with water. Speaking Rain ducked into the tepee and came out with a small basket with a lid. She scooped out a handful of the precious crushed rose-hip fruits they had gathered the fall before, then placed them in a wooden cup. Kaya put the hot stones in the water basket and stirred them. When the water was boiling, she poured it over the pink and orange hips.

"An aunt we've never met," Kaya said. "That hasn't happened before."

"Maybe she'll have some new basket patterns to teach us," Speaking Rain said.

"She might have new stories to tell us also," Kaya agreed. "I think it will be exciting to have a new family member, don't you?" She spoke boldly, ignoring the little twinge of apprehension in her stomach.

She carefully set the full cup on the hard ground by the fire to steep. When Tall Branch arrived, they could quickly heat the tea again so it would be just right. She smiled to herself at the thought of how pleased Tall Branch would be to see the steaming cup ready for her.

Kautsa walked out of the camp to see if the scouts were coming while Kaya and Speaking Rain helped Eetsa mash salmon for a special meal to be served soon after Tall Branch arrived. Eetsa seemed unusually intent on the task, using the big mortar and pestle to grind the dried salmon especially fine. The whole camp, in fact, wore an expectant air.

"Eetsa, this salmon is ground so fine, Tall Branch will think it's powder," Kaya said.

Her mother put down the pestle, her cheeks flushed from exertion. "Your aunt likes things to be just right. She will expect the salmon ground very fine."

"I see," Kaya said slowly. Just what kind of person was this Tall Branch? But her musings were interrupted as Kautsa came hurrying over.

"The scout says that our visitors are almost here," Kautsa said. "Will you and Speaking Rain go out to meet them and lead them into camp?"

Kaya swallowed. It looked like she was about to find out.

chapter 3

Tall Branch's Arrival

TALKING AND LAUGHING, Kaya, Speaking
Rain, and their cousins ran to the edge of the camp
with the elders following more slowly behind. Then
they waited in anticipation as the figures of four riders
appeared over the crest of a small rise, with the sparkling blue sky soaring over them. As they drew nearer,
Kaya saw that one rider was Toe-ta on his bay stallion,
Runner, escorting the visitors.

"A woman is riding a white horse," Kaya murmured to Speaking Rain. "That must be Tall Branch.
She wears a beautiful white dress, and she's tall and
strong looking. She holds the reins with pride." Two
men rode with the woman, one on either side. As the
riders drew closer, excited murmurs filled the air and
barking dogs raced out to the strange horses.

25

"Is that our new aunt? Is it?" Wing Feather and Sparrow pulled at Kaya's sleeve.

"It is," Kaya explained, bending down. "And her escorts, too."

The twins shouted with excitement and ran forward with a group of other children to surround the visitors and help bring them into camp.

As the party came closer, Kaya caught her breath. "Speaking Rain, what a beautiful horse Tall Branch is riding! It's white, with brown spots on the rump—the spots are in a cluster, almost like the shape of a star. I've never seen a pattern like that." The horse's mane was beautifully clean and groomed, and her tail was sparkling white. She pranced as she approached the group, her nostrils wide and her ears pricked forward.

The riders pulled up in a small cloud of dust and dismounted. The tall woman swept off her horse, the fringe on her dress dancing. The white deerskin was decorated with many elk's teeth, Kaya saw, and three glittering red beads. She was taller than Eetsa and broader across the shoulders, powerful looking. Her eyes swept the crowd waiting to greet her, and she inclined her head, acknowledging all of them.

Eetsa stepped forward to greet the riders. "You are all welcome here," she said. She smiled at Tall Branch. "Sister, we welcome you to your new home. It's been many years since we've lived in the same camp."

Tall Branch inclined her head. "I am grateful to be with you again, Sister," she said. But she did not smile. Her eyes examined each person in turn as Eetsa introduced the members of their band.

"I could lead your horse to the camp, Aunt," Kaya volunteered once the introductions were complete. She reached for the reins in Tall Branch's hand, but the mare threw up her head in surprise.

"Be careful!" Tall Branch snapped. "Spotted Star is high-strung. She doesn't like sudden movements. A girl your age should know how to approach a new horse."

Eetsa shot a concerned look at her sister. Kaya dropped her hand in surprise and stood silently, stung.

No one said anything. Kaya's face was hot. Then she felt Speaking Rain's hand steal into hers and squeeze.

Eetsa cleared her throat. "You are tired after your journey, Sister. Let us make you and your escorts comfortable." She led the procession into the circle of tepees, with Wing Feather and Sparrow dancing alongside, their toy bows and arrows clutched in their hands.

"Your tea will be perfect," Speaking Rain whispered to Kaya as they followed near the back. "What a good idea it was to make it."

"Katsee-yow-yow, Sister," Kaya said gratefully. As usual, her heart was soothed by Speaking Rain's soft words.

Outside of Kaya's family's tepee, Eetsa settled Tall Branch and her escorts on mats. Rabbit tied Spotted Star just beyond the circle of tepees and then brought her water. The twins scampered off behind the tepee, shouting to each other. Tall Branch arranged the folds of her white dress. She brushed the dirt from her skirt and smoothed it out.

"How was your journey, Sister?" Eetsa asked, laying her hand on Tall Branch's knee.

"The bog makes this journey long. We had to ride around its edges for a whole morning," Tall Branch said. Her face was lined with fatigue.

The bog! Kaya shivered a little at her aunt's words. For as long as she could remember, she'd known there was a big bog near the prairie. It stretched for a long way and plants grew there that grew nowhere else. Tall Branch's camp lay just on the other side of it, but Kaya's band did not go into the bog. To reach the other camp, they had a long ride around the edges of the bog instead. No rider would wish to ride *through* the bog. It had strange mists and winds that could confuse a traveler. Its quicksand could trap a walker or even a horse and hold her fast. Men had gone into the bog and never come out.

Kaya shivered again at the thought of quicksand sucking at her legs. She pushed the image away and leaned over. "May I serve Tall Branch the tea I made for her?" she whispered to her mother.

Eetsa smiled. "Of course. That will refresh her."

At the cooking fire, Kaya quickly reheated the tea with a couple of the hot stones, then took them out and balanced the steaming cup in both hands. The hot, fragrant water lapped at the brim as she walked up to Tall Branch. The older woman looked up.

"I made you this tea, Aunt—" Kaya began, but the words were barely out of her mouth when behind her Sparrow called in dismay, "My arrow!"

Kaya twisted around just as a small toy arrow zinged past her face, right toward Speaking Rain. Kaya swiped at the arrow to keep it from hitting her sister. The bright red tea sloshed from the cup and splashed onto Tall Branch's lovely white dress. Kaya's stomach did a sickening flip-flop.

"Oh, oh!" Tall Branch leaped to her feet. "My dress!"

"I'm sorry!" Kaya cried. "I'll—I'll wipe it off." She looked around for a piece of deerskin.

"I will do it." Tall Branch stood, her brows drawn

together. She glared at Sparrow, who was standing with his eyes fixed on the ground.

"I'm sorry," he whispered, his little voice even littler than usual.

Tall Branch acknowledged the apology with a frosty nod. Then she turned to Kaya. "You can set that cup down. I never cared much for rose-hip tea." She bent and disappeared into the tepee, leaving Kaya holding the now-empty cup—and feeling just as empty inside. Whatever had just happened, she was quite sure she had *not* succeeded in welcoming her stern new aunt.

Eetsa and Kautsa cleaned up Tall Branch's stained dress as best they could, and Sparrow was scolded for shooting his arrows so close to the tepee. The escorts and their horses had had their refreshments and taken their leave. Kaya and Speaking Rain led Spotted Star out to the herd pastured a short way from camp, with Kaya holding the lead rope and Speaking Rain holding Spotted Star's halter from the other side.

"I don't think Tall Branch likes me," Kaya confessed

to Speaking Rain. The words were hard to say. No one in their band had ever actually *disliked* her before.

"No, I don't think that can be right," her sister said. "She doesn't even know you."

"I know, but I've annoyed her twice." Kaya sighed.

Spotted Star jumped suddenly and gave a little prance, though the herd was still a ways off and no danger was near. "Calm down, Spotted Star!" Speaking Rain patted the horse's neck and spoke softly. But the mare kept her head up, her ears swiveling for new sounds. "This horse *is* nervous, as Tall Branch said."

Kaya could feel the mare's tension through the lead rope. "Shh, girl," she soothed, patting the horse's quivering neck. Her coat there was damp; she was sweating from nervousness.

As the girls approached the herd with the new arrival, the horses nearest them looked up from their grazing and pricked their ears. Steps High lifted her head and sniffed the air, scenting Spotted Star's presence. The horses were all fat and glossy from the abundant grass of the Weippe Prairie. They were a riot of black, brown, chestnut, white, and gray against the dark green and gold grasses. Tails switched, brushing away the flies, and jaws champed bits of grass as they watched the girls through big, dark-lashed eyes.

At the far edge of the herd, two of Kaya's cousins, Raven and Fox Tail, were guarding the herd on their horses. They were throwing sticks up in the air, trying to hit tree branches, but they saw Spotted Star and lifted their arms to acknowledge her arrival.

Steps High whinnied to Kaya and trotted forward to greet her. "There you are, my beautiful horse," Kaya said, stroking her black neck. "I've brought you a new friend. Be kind to her."

Speaking Rain kept a tight hold on Spotted Star's lead rope as the two horses snuffled each other's breath. Suddenly, Steps High flattened her ears and with a warning squeal dove in to nip Spotted Star's neck. The other horse reared back, eyes wide, jerking Speaking Rain with her.

"Steps High!" Kaya shouldered her way in front of her horse. "I know you want to be in charge, but Spotted Star is your guest. She just wants to eat." She gave Steps High a stern look.

"We should let Spotted Star graze over by the woods," Speaking Rain said. "The other horses will accept her better if she's not too near them at first."

"Good idea," Kaya said. "She will ease into the herd better if the others don't feel she's trying to push in."

They led the mare through the dry grass toward the woods at the edge of the meadow, and Speaking Rain removed Spotted Star's halter. The horse cantered off a few strides, her white tail held high, then stopped and stood still, watching the herd. Finally, she lowered her head to the grass.

"She's started to graze now," Kaya told Speaking Rain. "I think she'll be all right."

As Kaya turned toward camp, she thought she glimpsed a flash of silver moving through the woods—just for a moment, as quick as a glint of sunlight on water. She paused for a closer look.

"What is it, Kaya?" Speaking Rain asked.

Kaya studied the shadowy woods for a moment. "I thought I saw something moving, but I must have been mistaken. It's gone now."

Both girls were silent, straining to listen; then Speaking Rain inhaled sharply. "Something rustled, just now. Maybe we should go look." She moved toward the dark trees.

Kaya didn't want to go into the dark woods. She wanted to go back to the camp, to the food and fire and people there. "Aa-heh, let's look," she said, trying to sound bold.

Kaya led Speaking Rain to the edge of the meadow and stepped into the woods. The sheltering branches arched over them. The grass was shorter here, and softer. Both girls stood still. The silence was heavy, Kaya thought, like a wet deerskin pressing down on them. Her scalp prickled. She caught her breath. Was that a movement behind those shrubs—or was it just a flash of sunlight through fluttering leaves? She wasn't sure. A twig snapped behind them and she whirled around, the blood pounding in her ears. Nothing was there.

All the stories she'd heard of spirits and Stick People flashed through her mind. Sometimes, the legends said, dark spirits visited the world of people because they were displeased, or wanted to take things for themselves. Kaya moistened her suddenly dry lips.

They waited a moment longer, but the woods remained still. "We must have been imagining things," she whispered to Speaking Rain. "Come on. Let's go."

But as they waded out into the golden meadow and the comforting shuffling of the herd, Kaya felt sure that she hadn't imagined the odd silvery flash. Whether it was of this world or the spirit world, though—she didn't know.

chapter 4

A Shadowy Legend

THE SUN BEAT down on the camas field the next morning as the women and girls of Kaya's band harvested the roots. Along with Kautsa, Eetsa, and Tall Branch, Kaya poked the point of her digging stick into the hard ground with one hand and grasped the top of the camas plant with the other hand. She pried the bulbous brown-and-white root from the soil and shook off the dirt. Speaking Rain sat beside Kaya, piling the freshly dug roots into a large basket.

But Kaya was not focused on the roots, as Kautsa had told her she should be. Instead, her mind was full of the mysterious silvery flash in the woods. Had it been just a trick of the light? Or was it a spirit, showing itself?

All around her, women and girls were bent double, digging the camas roots, as they had done for the last several weeks. Today or tomorrow, they would finish the harvest. Already the dug roots were being peeled, cleaned, and slowly roasted in the big pits the women had dug in the ground. The roasting dried out the roots so that they would not spoil and could be kept for food through the long winter that was fast approaching.

Right now, though, the winter felt far away. Rain had fallen during the night, and the air was warm and heavy. Kaya sat back on her heels for a moment to rest. She saw Tall Branch glance at her sharply and hastily picked up her stick again. She didn't want Tall Branch to think she was a poor worker, not after yesterday's tea incident.

Tall Branch eyed Kaya for a moment longer, then returned to her digging, her stick efficiently prying up root after root, but carefully leaving every third or fourth plant. That way there would be roots for next year's harvest. Her mouth was set in a straight, firm line and her jaw was clenched. She had not spoken to Kaya or Speaking Rain this morning except for a brief

"Tawts may-we." Kaya noticed that Eetsa had placed herself next to Tall Branch. Now and then her mother spoke quietly to Tall Branch. Kaya thought it looked as if Eetsa were offering words of comfort.

Kaya missed Brown Deer in the camas fields. Her older sister had married last winter and gone to live with her husband's family. *At least I still have another sister with me,* she thought, glancing at Speaking Rain. But her sister was quiet and distant this morning. Kaya wondered if she was thinking about her dream of riding her beautiful horse.

"My little boy told me something strange this morning," a young woman named Yellow Flower said as she worked. The other women looked at her expectantly, though their hands never stopped moving. They often told news and stories while they dug. "On his way back from bathing in the river, he was walking out to the horse herd to bring the guards water after their night's watch. He said that as he approached the herd, he saw something at the edge of the woods. He thought it might be a horse, or maybe even just the shadow of a horse. But when he took a step closer, it vanished as if it were made of air. He watched for a while, but he didn't see it again." Yellow Flower widened her eyes dramatically.

Kaya's heart stood in her mouth. The digging stick dropped from her slack hand. Yellow Flower's son must have seen the same thing she had. She knew she hadn't imagined that silvery flash! Kautsa shot a look at Kaya's idle hands, and Kaya hastily picked up her stick and dug it into the dirt. She kept her eyes on her work, but her ears felt stretched as large as a jackrabbit's as she waited to hear what the others would say.

"Perhaps he saw one of the Ghost Wind Stallions," Kautsa said to Yellow Flower, smiling as if she was only half serious. She paused to pile dug roots into a large basket. "It's an old legend—do you know it?"

The women shifted down to another patch of ground. "I don't know the legend, Kautsa," Speaking Rain said.

"I will tell you." Kautsa's hands moved steadily, prying roots from the soil. "Long ago, the story says, a great canoe came to the shores of the sea that lies to the west of Nimíipuu country. The ship was from another land, far away. Nimíipuu traders stood on the shore. They saw a signal from the strange people on the ship. Then the traders saw horses swimming from the ship, their heads above the gray, churning water. The horses reached shore. They climbed onto the beach, water streaming from their backs. The traders received these creatures with awe. They were stallions, big and powerful. Their heads were high and their eyes looked back at you. They were silver, with black markings on their bodies and faces.

"The traders brought the stallions to Nimíipuu country. The Nimíipuu called them the Ghost Wind Stallions. They had powerful medicine; their connection to the spirit world was very strong. When they were bred to the mares of the Nimíipuu, they passed this medicine to their young.

"Some say that Nimíipuu horses carry the blood of the Ghost Wind Stallions. But the silver color has never been seen in our herds—at least, not in the elders' memory. The old ones say that a few horses still roam who have the strong medicine of the Ghost Wind Stallions. They too are beautiful, strong, and fast, with that ghostly silver color. Their hooves don't touch the ground when they run. They disappear into the fog and through the rain, evading all who try to capture them. Do they want something from the world of humans? We Nimíipuu don't know. Why do they sometimes appear among us? What do the Ghost Wind Stallions want from us?"

Kautsa stopped and smiled. "Some think Ghost Wind Stallions may still roam Nimíipuu country. But some think this story is just a story."

Kaya realized her mouth was hanging open a little. "What do you think, Kautsa?"

Her grandmother glanced at Kaya's idle digging stick. "I think it is time we dig roots."

"Oh, of course," Kaya said hastily and dug her stick into the ground, keeping her head down so that her grandmother couldn't see her face. *A ghost horse. A mythical stallion that no one can capture.* A prickle ran down her spine as she saw once more, in her mind's eye, the silver shape flashing among the dark trees. Had she truly seen a spirit yesterday? She dug blindly at a root, then peered down at the sudden dampness she felt on her palm. She had split the root with her digging stick.

"You are not treating the roots with respect."

Kaya's head snapped up. Tall Branch was standing over her, her own digging stick in her hand. Speaking Rain froze also. Kaya felt her sister's body tense. "Careless digging wastes the roots." Tall Branch's voice was loud, and other diggers looked over at Kaya and Speaking Rain.

Kaya flushed. "I do not want to disrespect the roots," she said, low.

"You are not paying attention to your work,"

Tall Branch lectured while everyone listened. "You are daydreaming over here, ignoring the roots." Her voice was shrill and her hands were knotted tightly on her hips, the digging stick jutting out from one fist. "When I was a girl, I never let gossip take me from my work. My greatest honor was to feed my people."

Kaya put her head down and dug fast. Her face was burning—and her heart was burning inside. She knew she needed to respect Tall Branch as her elder, but was she really not working hard? She had only damaged one root. Kaya struggled to quell the anger that welled in her. She swallowed hard. Tall Branch was a strong tribeswoman—she knew how to help the people. That's what Kautsa had said. So why did it feel as if her aunt had taken a dislike to her—and for no good reason?

Tall Branch had moved away, but her voice still floated over to Kaya. Now she was complaining about Spotted Star's place in the herd. "And the horse called Steps High won't let her drink. I saw that mare nip

Spotted Star, and now she has a wound on her rump. That horse should be trained better."

Kaya's fingers tightened on her digging stick. Now Tall Branch was criticizing her horse, too! Then Eetsa knelt beside Kaya and piled the roots Kaya had dug into her own basket. She smiled gently at Kaya, the same calm smile she always had. "Try to be patient with my sister. Her spirit is troubled just now." She rose, balancing the basket on her hip, and strode away across the camas field. Kaya watched her mother go and let out a long breath, trying to relax.

"She's right, of course," Speaking Rain said quietly. "You're a good worker. Everyone knows that."

Her sister's words spread like sage balm over Kaya's wounded soul. "Katsee-yow-yow," she whispered, and dug faster.

The sun was a pale disk overhead, burning faintly through the thick white clouds, when the women left the root fields and walked back to the tepees to rest and eat the midday meal. They carried big baskets and bags brimming with roots.

Back at the camp, Kautsa quickly set about building up the fire outside their tepee, to boil water to cook some chunks of dried salmon they had harvested last spring at Celilo Falls. Wing Feather and Sparrow had gone with Toe-ta to scout the location of an elk herd that had recently been spotted. Elk meat would be a treat at this time of year.

"Kaya," Kautsa said, "please ride out with Speaking Rain and collect firewood. We are running low."

"Aa-heh, we'll go," Kaya said. Speaking Rain nodded. They'd ride into the woods near the horse meadow, Kaya thought. They'd find plenty of firewood there. And maybe, whatever she had seen would show itself. A little shiver ran up and down Kaya's neck.

As Kaya and Speaking Rain hurried along the path to the herd pasture, they met Tall Branch coming back on the same path. She must have been visiting Spotted

Star. She eyed them. "Where are you two sneaking off to?"

"Kautsa wants us to get firewood," Kaya told her. She made sure that her voice was low and respectful.

Tall Branch nodded grudgingly, but she stood and watched them as they passed by her.

After catching and saddling their horses, Kaya and Speaking Rain rode out of the herd clearing, Kaya on Steps High and Speaking Rain on the quiet gray mare she'd been riding recently. When Kaya took up the leading rein she always used to guide Speaking Rain's horse, she heard Speaking Rain sigh.

"You're thinking about your dream," Kaya said, looking over her shoulder at Speaking Rain. She had almost forgotten about Speaking Rain's sleepwalking. Her sister sat gracefully on the mare, holding her reins steady. But her face was a mask of sadness.

"I am," Speaking Rain admitted. "I can't seem to let it float away. But forget it, Kaya. It's a silly dream that will never be anything more." She set her jaw.

Kaya knew not to ask more questions just now.

The weather had shifted and now clouds covered the sky more thickly, promising rain. They brushed through the tall grasses of the herd meadow. Kaya guided the horses into the woods at the spot where she'd seen the odd flash yesterday.

The air was cooler in the woods, and mist hung amid the trees. Branches and bushes loomed up like ghosts, then floated away. The smell of damp and dead leaves hung in the air.

All thoughts of firewood gone, Kaya peered through the dimness. She wanted to see the strange shape again—and she didn't want to.

"There it is!" she yelped, twisting around to face Speaking Rain. "I saw something—a silver flash like yesterday, but this time it seemed as large as a horse!" She looked back toward the deep woods. The shape was gone.

Kaya swallowed, trying to moisten her dry mouth. "Here, let's go investigate." She urged Steps High forward and Speaking Rain followed. With every step deeper into the woods, Kaya ached to turn back. She didn't want to meet a ghost, but she was burning with curiosity.

Then something moving among the trees caught her eye. Now Kaya could see the shape clearly. It was the silhouette of a horse, a dark outline in the mist, powerful, delicate. The shape moved behind a massive oak tree and was gone.

"Kaya! Do you see it again? I feel as if something's here," Speaking Rain said.

Kaya thought her heart would pound out of her chest. "It—it *looked* like a horse. But it was so silent." The unearthly smooth gliding of the shape had unnerved her. The Ghost Wind Stallions of the legend crossed her mind. "Do—do you think it could be a spirit?"

Speaking Rain didn't answer for a moment. She was holding herself taut, as if she were listening with every fiber. "No," she whispered finally. "I think

I feel hoofbeats, deeper in the woods—as faint as a heartbeat."

Kaya tried to listen too, but she heard nothing. The woods were strangely quiet. Even the birds did not sing. Just the dark tree trunks, standing silently in the curling mist. Kaya had the feeling that something was watching them. She threw a sharp glance over her shoulder.

Nothing.

"Do you see hoofprints?" Speaking Rain asked. Her face was oddly intense. "Perhaps we could track him."

Kaya swallowed. "Maybe we should go back. What if it *is* a spirit? We don't always know the intentions of spirits. Think of the Stick People. Sometimes they do harm, sometimes they—"

"No!" Speaking Rain snapped.

Kaya started. Speaking Rain's cloudy eyes were wide. They seemed almost to see into the mist. "Take me to where you saw him," Speaking Rain said, softly now, but firmly.

Her hands sweaty on the reins, Kaya led Speaking

Rain deeper into the trees. She halted at the massive oak. "This is where I lost sight of him," she said.

They dismounted, looping the horses' reins over a low tree branch. The ground was soft and loamy under Kaya's moccasins. Kaya scanned the ground, which was covered by a dense layer of tough oak leaves. "Anything?" Speaking Rain whispered.

Kaya knelt to look more closely. Leaves, earth, moss. "No hoofprints," she murmured. Her scalp crawled as she spoke.

Ghosts left no prints, of course.

Kaya suddenly became aware of how deep the shadows were under the trees. "We have to get firewood. The others are waiting." Her voice sounded too loud in the hush of the woods. Speaking Rain nodded, and quickly the two girls remounted and trotted out of the trees. Kaya exhaled as they left the woods behind.

chapter 5
The Ghost Horse

THAT NIGHT, TUCKED into her warm skins, Kaya could think of nothing but the misty woods, the silver shadow, the horse-shape that moved without making a sound. Was it a spirit, a ghost horse? What was it doing, slipping through the woods, showing itself to people? What did it want? The medicine woman Bear Blanket had sometimes spoken of evil spirits. And— a new, unwelcome thought pushed its way into Kaya's mind—why had it appeared just as Tall Branch came to their camp? Their aunt had traveled by the bog. Had the spirit come out of the bog and followed her?

Kaya squeezed her eyes shut and snuggled closer to Speaking Rain. Her sister shifted in their furs. "Are you awake?" Kaya whispered.

"Aa-heh," Speaking Rain murmured. "I keep

thinking about what we found in the woods."

"You mean, *didn't* find," Kaya reminded her.

Speaking Rain opened her eyes. "You're worried he's a spirit, but I felt his hoofbeats through the ground."

"If he's real, why didn't he leave hoofprints?" Kaya insisted in a whisper. "The ground was soft."

"And covered with tough oak leaves. Perhaps they hid his prints." Suddenly, Speaking Rain raised up on her elbow. "I want to search for him again tomorrow." In the faint moonlight from the smokehole Kaya saw that her sister's face was set with determination.

Kaya's heart sank. "Perhaps we should consult Kautsa and Bear Blanket first—"

"There's no need, Kaya. He's real. I know it in my heart." Speaking Rain lay back on the furs and closed her eyes. The decision had been made, Kaya could see.

Kaya lay back too and stared at the darkness behind her eyelids. Her sister was sure the strange silver horse wasn't a ghost. But what if Speaking Rain was wrong?

...

The next morning before root digging, Kaya and Speaking Rain padded past the horse herd and entered the woods. The mist had lifted, but the smell of damp and loamy rot hung in the air. They had decided not to ride this time. It would be easier to track the ghost horse on foot—if they *could* track him, Kaya thought.

Speaking Rain strode close behind Kaya, holding a pinch of her dress. A small, excited smile turned up the corners of her mouth. "Let's go back to the oak tree where you saw him yesterday."

Kaya almost jumped at her sister's voice. She felt as if every muscle in her body was stretched taut as a bowstring.

"We should search the ground more carefully," Speaking Rain went on.

Once they were among the trees, the thick, late-summer leaves closed in around them and the sunlight dimmed. Their moccasins were silent on the mossy ground. Softly, the sisters crept deeper into the woods, Speaking Rain following close behind Kaya, brushing away twigs and branches with an outstretched hand.

A small stream trickled among the trees, choked with twigs and clots of dead leaves. Kaya turned to help her sister. "Here, take a big step—"

Suddenly, something exploded out of the ground in front of them. Kaya stifled a scream and Speaking Rain clutched her. "What was that?" Speaking Rain whispered. "It sounded like a grouse."

A grouse—of course! The small brown birds roosted in the bushes and flew straight up in a panic when people or animals approached. Kaya gave a weak laugh and tried to control her shaky knees. "I must be really on edge to be startled by a grouse."

Kaya's heart was still pounding as she led her sister on to the big oak where she'd last seen the silver horse-shape.

They knelt down. Kaya examined the thick carpet of oak leaves that covered the ground, looking again for any sign that the horse had passed this way. Speaking Rain touched the tree trunk to determine how far away from it she was and then felt over the area around it with her delicate fingertips.

After a moment, Kaya sat back on her heels. She couldn't see any trace of the horse. There was nothing to track. She rose to her feet. The root digging would be starting soon. They should get back to camp.

Then she noticed that Speaking Rain was picking up the tough, leathery oak leaves and piling them to one side. As Kaya watched, puzzled, her sister ran her fingers over a depression in the damp dirt she had uncovered. "I knew it was real," Speaking Rain murmured, almost to herself. "I knew we would find it."

Kaya bent over to see. There, pressed into the dirt, was a faint half-moon shape. A hoofprint.

"It *has* left a trail," Kaya breathed. Relief washed over her. The silver horse was not a spirit. He was real.

Speaking Rain pushed aside more leaves, exploring the soft earth with her fingertips. "And here's another."

"And here!" Kaya spotted another hoofprint in the mossy earth farther from the tree. "And another." She stood up and examined the ground, walking slowly. "Here, the trail leads this way."

Kaya led Speaking Rain deeper into the woods, following the faint trail. Boulders began to appear among the trees, poking gray shoulders up from the ground.

"The prints are clearer here," Kaya told Speaking Rain. "The horse was trotting around the boulders." She could tell the horse's gait from the way the prints were doubled up and evenly spaced in two straight lines.

"Where was he going, I wonder?" Speaking Rain's face was alight with excitement. Kaya couldn't help feeling a little of the thrill, too.

"I don't know, but remember that rocky place a little farther along?" Kaya asked. "That's the way the tracks seem to be heading."

The ground was growing stonier. Plates of rock now replaced soil in some places, and pebbles and stones as large as fists covered the path. Kaya squinted at the ground and slowed their pace. Rocks were tumbled everywhere. She could no longer see where the horse had stepped; the ground was too stony. She searched the landscape for any clue—a clump of horsehair stuck in bark, a broken branch.

Rocks—and nothing else. Kaya sighed. "I've lost him. I'm sorry, Speaking Rain."

Her sister laid a soft hand on her arm. "You really tried, Kaya. Katsee-yow-yow for that. You—" Speaking Rain stopped.

Kaya saw her face grow alert. "What?" she asked. "What is it?"

"Shh!" Speaking Rain raised her hand. *"He's here."*

"Where?" Kaya looked around. "How do you know?"

"I just know. He's here." Speaking Rain's eyes stared into the distance. She sniffed the air. Her body trembled. "Turn around."

An eerie feeling passed over Kaya. Slowly, she turned.

A massive silver stallion was standing not ten strides away.

chapter 6

The Stallion's Secret

THE STALLION STOOD looking at them, backed up against tall gray rocks that rose up behind him and stretched to both sides. His body, mane, and tail were a silvery shade Kaya had never seen before, the coat studded with brilliant black spots. His deep brown eyes were huge and alert, fixed on the girls. His head was raised high, his ears pricked together, almost meeting over his small, delicate head.

The stallion's body was tense, trembling like leaves in spring, and he was thin. "Oh, Speaking Rain! He must be hungry. His ribs and his hipbones stick out," Kaya murmured. "But his face is proud. He's not afraid of us."

"No," Speaking Rain said. "I know." Kaya looked at her sister in surprise.

"I can sense him," Speaking Rain said, almost more to herself than to Kaya. She took a step toward the stallion, her hands outstretched. Drops of mist glimmered in her hair like jewels.

The stallion snorted as she took another step closer.

"Speaking Rain, wait," Kaya whispered. Stallions could be dangerous. Toe-ta didn't allow children to handle them. They were very strong, but more than that, they could be unpredictable and short-tempered. And this one looked just like the Ghost Wind Stallions of legend. Did he have powerful medicine too? And if so, what did he want to use it for—good . . . or something else?

Her sister did not seem to hear her. Speaking Rain took another step. Kaya could see her reaching with every fiber toward the horse. He eyed her, snorted, and pinned his ears, a caution sign. He pranced in place and whickered a warning.

"He'll run!" Kaya said.

"Let him run." Speaking Rain's voice floated in the heavy air. "I can smell his fear. I can hear how rapidly he breathes."

Kaya smelled only the stallion's damp coat and the trees and leaves around her.

"Go," Speaking Rain said to the stallion. "I know you need to flee. It's all right. We'll meet each other again."

The stallion's hooves came to rest. He was still. His ears swiveled to catch Speaking Rain's words. Kaya held her breath.

Then Speaking Rain smiled, and as if she had released him, the stallion galloped past them in a sweaty flash of silver fur and black spots.

He ran into the woods, swallowed up instantly by the mist. Speaking Rain stood, facing the direction he'd run. If she didn't know better, Kaya could have sworn that her sister was watching him go.

...

Now that they had met the stallion, they could think of nothing else. After their morning bath in the river, they offered to go out and fetch firewood, so they could see him. The sun was burning pink in the eastern sky the next morning when they left camp. Riding this time, they returned to the rocky alcove and tracked the stallion's hoofprints. This time his trail was easy to follow. It led them from the alcove to a small clearing where he was grazing.

His brilliant black spots stood out among the soft silver-greens and browns of the trees and dewy grasses. He *did* look like a creature from the world of spirits, Kaya thought. He raised his head at their approach, watching them.

They halted their horses a short distance away and dismounted, tying Steps High and Speaking Rain's gray mare to trees within easy reach of grass.

"Tawts may-we, friend," Speaking Rain said. Her voice was calm and confident. The Ghost Wind Stallion watched her as she walked toward him.

Kaya caught her sister's sleeve. "Wait. Let's not get too close yet, or he may run again."

Speaking Rain paused, then smiled at Kaya. "You are a skilled horsewoman, Sister," she said, "but the rules are different with this one—I just know. He's lonely."

She walked up to the stallion with complete assurance, discerning his location from his breathing and his small movements.

"I am glad to meet you," she told him. He watched her, snorting a little, tense but not moving. His muscles stood out like rope under his skin.

Kaya froze as her sister quietly placed her hand on the stallion's neck. The whole world hung in the balance. He could bolt. Or he could stay.

For a long moment, no one, human or animal, moved. The clearing was silent.

The stallion turned his head. He snuffled at Speaking Rain, blowing deeply through his nose to take in her scent. She lifted her hand, stroked his neck.

He turned his head away. His neck relaxed. His ears swiveled slightly.

Kaya let out the breath she didn't realize she'd been holding. Her knees suddenly felt trembly.

Speaking Rain continued stroking the stallion's silver-gray coat. "Come," she said to Kaya over her shoulder. "Come meet him."

A new note in her voice struck Kaya. It was the first time, she thought, that her sister had invited *her* to experience something new. For the first time that Kaya could remember, Speaking Rain was the leader. Kaya had to trust and follow her, just as Speaking Rain had always trusted and followed Kaya.

Trying to mimic her sister's calm confidence, Kaya held her hand near the stallion's muzzle, the way she'd been taught. Standing this close, she felt power radiating from him, thin though he was. His neck arched proudly, his long, shaggy forelock falling over his huge, clear brown eyes. His back was straight, his legs long and clean, with small, delicate hooves.

The stallion made no move to run. He allowed them to stand close to him, running their hands down his neck in the warmth under his heavy silver mane.

"There now, you're relaxing," Speaking Rain murmured to him. "Kaya, he's really gentle, I think. See how he's leaning into my hand when I scratch him? But where is your herd, Ghost? Why are you wandering alone, and so thin? Tell us your secrets— then we can help you."

She dug her hand into the pouch at her waist and brought out a handful of dried huckleberries. Horses liked the sweet berries as much as people did. Ghost snuffled the berries delicately from Speaking Rain's open palm while she stroked his shoulder with the other hand. Kaya bent to pick up one that had dropped and offered it to him. The stiff whiskers that pricked his velvety muzzle tickled her hand, and she tentatively stroked his flat, broad cheek.

Suddenly, Speaking Rain caught her breath.

"What is it?" Kaya asked. Her sister's face was crumpled in distress.

"Oh, Kaya, he's been hurt." Speaking Rain's fingers felt up and down the stallion's shoulder. "Here."

Speaking Rain parted the hair and Kaya peered at the spot her sister indicated and sucked in her breath. Long wounds ran across the stallion's back and down his shoulder, partially hidden by his long, shaggy mane. They crisscrossed each other like the weaving of a basket, showing a glaring pink-red in the silver-and-black coat. Some wounds were partially healed, others open and weeping.

"Whip marks," Kaya breathed. She'd often seen the short, stiff whips that the Nimíipuu used to urge horses forward in races. But someone had used a whip for a different reason—to beat this horse cruelly.

"Aa-heh," Speaking Rain said. "And here on his rump are healed marks, made long ago." Her fingers traced the long raised welts. "But the wounds on his shoulders are fresh. Someone has hurt this horse many times, perhaps for a long time." Her voice was full of pain. The stallion shivered his skin as she touched the marks, but he didn't move away.

"I have heard of this sort of thing happening," Kaya said. She reached toward Ghost's ears to pet them, but he jerked his head up and away, his eyes widening momentarily. "Ah, I'm sorry," she told him. "You're right. I'll move more slowly." Carefully but firmly, she patted his muzzle. His head relaxed again. "But he is so beautiful, Speaking Rain. I can't imagine someone wanting to hurt him."

Speaking Rain gently put her arms around Ghost's neck. Kaya could tell that she was moving with care, sensing if he was afraid of her, would jerk away. But he seemed almost to lean into her, as if he was waiting for attention—as if he was starved for it. "Toe-ta always says the Nimíipuus' horses are their brothers. But there must be someone who thinks that his horse is more like an old moccasin—to be torn up and thrown away."

The sun glinted through the trees, and Kaya looked up. "The sun is getting higher. Kautsa will be looking for us to dig roots." Something about the closeness between Ghost and Speaking Rain unsettled her. The horse almost seemed to have some kind of hold over her sister—one that did not seem quite of this world.

Speaking Rain gave Ghost one last squeeze. "We will be back," she told him firmly. "Wait for us." He watched them with his large dark eyes, as if he understood.

The girls untethered their horses and swung into the saddles. "Perhaps now we know why Ghost is alone," Speaking Rain said as they rode away, her horse led by Kaya's as always. "Perhaps he fled the owner who beat him. Maybe that's why he won't come near the camp."

"Ah, you must be right." A little ripple of excitement rose in Kaya—the mystery of Ghost was becoming clearer. "Perhaps he doesn't trust grown men. But he'll allow us near him!" She had heard of something similar happening with dogs. Long ago, a cousin had mistreated his dog by hitting him. The cousin had eventually left their camp, but the dog remained. After that, only women and girls could touch him, never men. Horses might be the same.

"Yet he's been near the herd," Kaya said thoughtfully. "He must want to be around other horses." She guided Steps High through a small stream, the water splashing up around her ankles.

"But he's different from them," Speaking Rain said, so quietly that Kaya had to strain to catch her words. "I know how that feels. I have felt different and alone my whole life." Something about her voice made Kaya turn sharply in her saddle to look at her sister.

"No!" Kaya halted Steps High alongside the gray mare. "You've never been alone. Nimíipuu always care for each other. We're sisters, aren't we?"

Speaking Rain sighed and smiled. She reached over and groped for Kaya's hand, squeezed it, and then let it go. "Sister, we are. And you have always taken good

care of me. But I *am* different; we both know that. I've
always had to be helped. Ghost and I—we both stand
apart from our groups."

"You understand Ghost so well, it's as if the two
of you have talked," Kaya teased gently. But a twinge
of unease touched her even as she spoke.

"Yes," Speaking Rain said, so quietly that the play-
ful smile left Kaya's lips. "It's as if we have. You know,
I feel that I've met him before. Remember my dream
from a few nights ago?"

Kaya remembered. A beautiful horse that Speaking
Rain galloped across the prairie alone. She shivered.
"Do . . . do you think your dream was a vision?" Or was
it a trick of some kind, sent from the spirit world? Sent
even to draw Speaking Rain astray? Kaya had always
taken care of her sister—it was her duty.

Speaking Rain paused for so long that Kaya
thought she had decided not to answer. "I don't know,"
she finally burst out. "But—oh, Kaya, what if it was?
What if I am meant to ride Ghost on my own?" She

clutched the gray mare's reins, her eyes wide and a spot of color in each cheek.

"I...I'm not sure," Kaya answered carefully. "I don't know enough of how to interpret visions. We should ask Bear Blanket."

"No," Speaking Rain said immediately. "Let's not tell anyone yet. Please, Kaya. I want to keep Ghost only for us—just for now. I think that's how he wants it."

chapter 7

"My Horse Is Gone"

AS SOON AS they arose the next morning, Kaya
and Speaking Rain prepared a thick mash of camas
root mixed with berries to take to Ghost. He needed
more food if they wanted him to get fatter. And
Speaking Rain had mixed a salve of bear fat and sage
leaves to put on his wounds. All day, they watched for
a chance to visit the stallion. But Eetsa needed their
help watching the twins, and then all afternoon the
women and girls worked hard together digging a new
roasting pit because the camas harvest had been so
bountiful.

Now Eetsa sat by the tepee, taking a brief rest
before starting to prepare the evening meal. Kaya saw
her chance. "May Speaking Rain and I go to visit Steps
High before we eat?" They might be able to find Ghost,

though they wouldn't be able to search far for him before they had to return. Still, over Eetsa's shoulder, Kaya could see Speaking Rain's face light up. *Katsee-yow-yow,* Speaking Rain mouthed. Kaya could tell Speaking Rain knew she was trying to find a way for them to visit Ghost.

Eetsa nodded. "Be back before the sun sets. And before you go, will you please rearrange Tall Branch's sleeping furs inside the tepee? She has said the draft through the bottom of the tepee is bothering her at night. Will you move her sleeping roll closer to the fire?"

"Aa-heh, I will," Kaya said.

As she and Speaking Rain turned to go, Tall Branch strode up to them. "Kaya, Speaking Rain, you should not leave when there is still work to do. You should help your mother prepare the meal." She raked the girls over with her sharp eyes, then walked away down the path that led to the root fields and the roasting pits.

Kaya's cheeks burned as she lowered her head and stared at her feet. No one else in the camp spoke to her the way Tall Branch did. She and Speaking Rain had always prided themselves on working hard for their people. To have someone tell them they were lazy was shameful—and a little unfair.

A firm hand on her back made her look up. "You have worked hard all day," Eetsa said to the girls. "I am glad to have such workers as you. I will prepare the meal." She paused. "Sometimes, people speak harshly. But it is their own pain that makes their words harsh." She gave the girls a little smile. "I think you know what I am saying."

The tight feeling in Kaya's chest loosened, and Speaking Rain smiled too. Eetsa understood. She didn't think they were bad workers. Kaya ducked inside the tepee. Speaking Rain stayed outside to help Eetsa.

Light filtered through chinks in the tule mats that covered the tepee, and inside all was peaceful and cool. Rolls of sleeping furs and mats were stacked neatly around the edges of the tepee, and baskets and raw-hide parfleches leaned against the poles. In the middle, within a circle of stones, the embers of this morning's fire smoldered, some of the coals still a deep rose red. Tall Branch's bundles were stacked near the entrance, and her white dress hung from a peg on one of the tepee's poles, the red stain from the rose-hip tea still visible. Kaya glanced at it and quickly looked away. She fought against the wave of irritation and impatience that rose in her chest.

Hastily, she pulled Tall Branch's heavy baskets from their spot near the fire beside Eetsa and Toe-ta's sleeping skin. She dragged Tall Branch's sleeping roll from the wall of the tepee and struggled to push it into place near the fire. "Ooh!" Kaya moaned. The white dress had fallen from its peg on the tepee pole. Kaya snatched it up and brushed at it, stumbling over something just behind her. She felt the thing shift, but she focused on rubbing out a smear of ash on the hem of the white dress. Hurriedly, she stuck the dress back on its peg and, without a backward look, slipped outside. She'd spent long enough in the tepee—she was nearly as anxious as Speaking Rain to see Ghost.

The sun was sending slanting golden rays through the pine trees as Kaya and Speaking Rain neared the herd. Kaya spotted Ghost almost immediately. "There he is!" she exclaimed. He was standing in the trees at the edge of the woods, watching a knot of mares grazing nearby. Kaya glanced quickly at the boys guarding the herd. They were on the far side of the meadow, trying to round up a young mare who had strayed into a thorn thicket. They were too far away to see clearly what was happening. What luck! She and Speaking Rain could visit with Ghost right here.

She was about to lead Speaking Rain closer to Ghost when she saw him amble out from the shelter of the trees. He lowered his head, pulled his ears back, and sniffed at the knot of mares. Spotted Star stood among them. She seemed especially alert, watching Ghost with her head high and her body tense. Then she lifted her tail and cantered in a tight circle. "Spotted Star is nervous," Kaya told Speaking Rain, describing what she had just seen. "Ghost wants company, but Spotted Star doesn't want him near."

Ghost left Spotted Star and galloped along the edge of the meadow, leaving the mares. Kaya caught her breath at the powerful action of his long legs and rippling muscles. His head was high, and his mane flew in the breeze. His tail rippled behind him like water. His feet barely seemed to touch the ground as he ran, and his coat shone like silver, the black spots like the smoothest river stones.

"Oh, Speaking Rain, he gallops like the wind!" Kaya breathed.

"I know," her sister said. "I can feel the rhythm of his hooves through the ground."

Ghost shifted his course and cantered into the trees.

"Come on!" Kaya cried. "He's going into the woods. Let's follow him!"

They ran after the stallion, stumbling over tussocks of grass. He was standing in a little grove of pine trees, nibbling the tips of the needles. He seemed tenser today, Kaya thought. He was shivering his coat, his tail slightly lifted, as though waiting for something to happen.

"Hello, Ghost," Speaking Rain said quietly, going toward him with her hand out. But Ghost tossed his head and whickered a warning, rolling his eyes so the whites showed.

"Watch out!" Kaya resisted the urge to pull Speaking Rain back.

Speaking Rain shook her head. "I want to keep trying to get to know him." She stepped forward. "Here, Ghost, we've brought you a treat." Her voice was calm, but Kaya could see her hand shaking just a little. Speaking Rain took another step.

The stallion ignored her. He nibbled another branch with his sensitive lips.

Another step.

"Speaking Rain." Kaya kept her voice deliberately low. "*Don't.*"

Speaking Rain laid her hand on the stallion's neck. "Hello," she said.

The stallion squealed, pinned his ears back flat, and quick as a snake whipped his head around. His bared teeth grazed her knuckles.

Speaking Rain stumbled back. Kaya gasped. Ghost eyed them both for another long minute. Kaya got the message: *I'm in charge here.* His eyes seemed bottomless. Kaya dropped her own gaze.

Speaking Rain put her hand to her mouth.

"Here, let me see." Kaya inspected the scrape. "It's not bleeding. But we should go back to camp now. He doesn't want us here. He hurt you!"

Speaking Rain set her jaw in her new, determined way. "He's trying to push us away because he doesn't trust us yet—that's all. And if we leave now, he never will."

Speaking Rain took the woven cover off the basket of mash. She set it on the ground near the stallion, not trying to touch him again but letting the delicious scent of the food reach his nose.

Speaking Rain stepped back and stood quietly, her head to one side, listening to his breathing. "Are you hungry, friend?" she asked him. Her voice was low and musical. She sounded as if he'd never tried to bite her, never received her with anything but affection and trust. She sounded—Kaya thought—as if she believed in him. Kaya wanted to believe in him too—but she couldn't help feeling wary. He had turned on Speaking Rain so quickly!

The stallion lowered his head and sniffed the basket. Both girls held absolutely still. He dipped his nose in and delicately ate some. Softly, Speaking Rain laid her hand on his neck again. This time, his ears stayed up. She ran her hand up and down his neck and onto his back. She patted his muzzle, buried deep in the basket and dripping with mash. Ghost let her.

With a huge smile, Speaking Rain turned to Kaya. "It's all right now. He says we can stay." Kaya exhaled, the tension running out of her shoulders.

They went to work. Speaking Rain rubbed the sage salve she'd made onto his wounds, and Kaya groomed his rough coat with a brush made of twigs tied together, pulling all the mud and burrs out, until his silver fur gleamed like a mirror. Ghost no longer shied from them. He slurped the mash in big gulps, then stood quietly.

Murmuring gently, Speaking Rain crouched down to rub his dry hooves with bear grease and scrape off mud. She massaged his legs with more of the grease and Ghost leaned toward her, his eyes half closed, almost trembling with ecstasy.

"There!" Speaking Rain finished rubbing Ghost's legs. With an air of having finished a job, she stood up and ran her hands along his face and neck, down to his now-silky mane, hanging as straight and smooth as Toe-ta's braids, lightly across his cleaned cuts, and

along his soft coat to his rump. Kaya stepped back
and admired him with her eyes as Speaking Rain did
with her hands. He was even more magnificent than
before, if that was possible. Just then, the setting sun
broke from behind the clouds and the last light filtered
through the pine trees, bathing the stallion in a cloud
of gold. Kaya caught her breath.

"Oh, Speaking Rain, he glitters when the sun
touches him. He shines like rippling water. He's as
beautiful as a meadowlark's singing."

Speaking Rain smiled and slid her hand under
Ghost's neck and up to his cheek on the other side,
cradling his head. He turned toward her, relaxing into
her touch, and Kaya watched as Speaking Rain gently
rested her forehead against his. They stayed that way
a long time, breathing each other's breath.

Speaking Rain didn't say a word during the walk
back to the camp. But she didn't have to. Kaya could
read her face: Her sister was in love.

They made their way back through the trees and

around the herd meadow to the path that led to camp. Speaking Rain floated beside Kaya, her cloudy eyes far away, a faint smile touching the corners of her mouth. Kaya wondered if her sister was going to soar away over the treetops like a hawk.

"Maybe I should tie a rope to your ankle," she teased as they neared the tepees. "You look as light as a bird. I'm worried that you might float away."

"I was thinking about Ghost," Speaking Rain admitted. "Kaya, do you think, if he learns to trust us, he might see that not everyone is like the man who hurt him? Maybe he might even learn to trust the others in our band, like Toe-ta. Then he could become a part of our herd, and stay with us—stay with me!" Her voice was dreamy. Then it grew serious. "He's so weak. He needs us."

Kaya swallowed. She thought of how Ghost's hipbones and ribs stuck out. Her sister was right. Ghost did need them.

"We'll find a way to help him. I know we will,"

she reassured Speaking Rain.

The camp looked oddly deserted as they came up to the circle of tepees. There were no little children running around the edges or women kneeling on their mats, banking the fires for the night. Outside Kaya's tepee, the fire was burning. Wing Feather and Sparrow's precious toy bows and arrows lay abandoned on the ground nearby. Then Kaya spotted everyone clustered in a group near her family's tepee.

Eetsa, Toe-ta, Tall Branch, and Kautsa turned around as the girls approached. Kaya stopped at the looks on their faces. Tall Branch's lips were pressed together in a thin, straight line. Kautsa's face was solemn. She stepped forward. "Tall Branch's sleeping furs have been burned. She found them in the tepee, lying partly in the coals of the fire."

"A hole in my bearskin as big as two fists," Tall Branch said tightly. "Put there by carelessness."

Kaya's mind spun, trying to figure out what they were talking about. Then her stomach dropped. She remembered bumping into something heavy as she'd rushed to leave the tepee—rushed to go visit Ghost. She must have bumped Tall Branch's sleeping roll right into the smoldering coals of the morning fire.

She moistened her lips, trying to think of what to say into the awful silence. Speaking Rain stepped closer to her side, so that Kaya could feel the warmth of her sister's arm against her own. That gave her the courage to say, "Tall Branch, forgive me. I was wrong to be so careless."

A heavy pause descended, and then Tall Branch jerked her head once, acknowledging Kaya's words. But Kaya could see from the harsh lines in her aunt's face that Tall Branch was far from forgiving her.

Just then, a young man named Jumps Back burst into camp. He ran straight for the group. He was breathing heavily and his face was flushed. Everyone turned toward him, immediately alert.

"What has happened?" Toe-ta asked.

Jumps Back rested his hands on his knees, catching

his breath. "I can't find Spotted Star in the herd. I fear she's missing."

"What?" Tall Branch stared at him, her eyes blazing. "What are you saying? How could you lose my horse?"

"Let us have calm," Toe-ta said. "Jumps Back, tell us what you know."

"Two other men and I were taking over the evening guard. I always look over the herd before I begin a watch. I looked especially for your mare," he said to Tall Branch, "since she was just introduced three days ago. But I could not find her in the herd or anywhere in the pasture. After looking thoroughly, I came directly here."

Tall Branch put her hands over her face. "My horse," she moaned. "My horse is gone." The strength had left her voice.

"We will ride out to search for the mare immediately," Toe-ta said. "We'll need a small party—those whose horses are tethered here near camp." His voice rang with authority and the group scattered, with

some running toward their horses and others returning to their cookfires or tending children.

Kaya nudged Speaking Rain and without a word,
they ran after the searchers as they rode off toward
the pastures.

chapter 8

Kaya Accused

TOE-TA, JUMPS BACK, Eetsa, Tall Branch, and some of the older boys quickly mounted horses tethered near the camp and trotted down the path in the waning light, those on foot coming behind. Kaya and Speaking Rain ran at the back of the group. The horse herd was spread out over the large meadow, peacefully grazing as they had been before. The golden light touched their backs; their tails swished against flies. As the group approached, a few of the near horses lifted their heads in surprise, still chewing, their ears pricked toward the riders.

"Those on foot, look for tracks," Toe-ta commanded. "Then all searchers fan out and look for any other signs of the mare."

Kaya scanned the ground around her. Tracking

would be difficult, she could see. The soft ground was thickly patterned with hoofprints, all blending together in a mass of half-moon shapes.

She couldn't help thinking of Ghost, somewhere back in the trees. So far, only she and Speaking Rain knew he existed. She could tell by Speaking Rain's furrowed brow and the way she kept biting her bottom lip that she was thinking the same thing.

The riders began to spread out, riding in sight of each other, circling the outskirts of the herd. Suddenly, a shriek rang across the meadow. "There! What was that?"

Kaya looked up to see Tall Branch astride her borrowed mare, pointing across the herd clearing toward the woods. For a split second, Kaya saw Ghost, standing like a silver sentinel among the trees.

Then, like a flash, he was gone, melting into the trees. A single low branch quivered, the only sign that he had ever been there.

"I saw him!" Kaya whispered to Speaking Rain.

Tall Branch rode closer to Toe-ta. "Whose stallion was that?" she asked him. "Why was he lurking in the trees?"

Toe-ta slowly shook his head. "He's not one of ours. He must be a wild rogue, hanging around."

"Wild stallions are nothing but trouble!" Tall Branch declared. "They fight the other stallions and steal mares. I know—it's a problem my band has dealt with for a long time. We must find him—*he* could have stolen Spotted Star. He might be hiding her now. We must find him and drive him away!" Her voice rang out over the group, and Speaking Rain let out a small gasp.

Kaya froze where she stood. Her eyes darted from her father to the other riders to the empty edges of the meadow. Would the riders track Ghost right now? He would be lost to Speaking Rain forever if men came after him with arrows and shouts.

But Toe-ta sat still on his big bay stallion, studying the herd meadow and the darkening woods. "Raven!"

he called. "Did you see any sign of this stallion during the afternoon watch?"

"No." Raven shook his head.

"And the horses were calm when we rode up. If a rogue stallion had cut into the herd and stolen a mare, our horses would certainly be agitated." Toe-ta studied the herd, thinking aloud. He turned to Tall Branch. "It seems unlikely that the stallion stole your horse, Sister." Kaya let out a sigh of relief. Beside her, she felt Speaking Rain relax too.

But Toe-ta was not finished. "However, you are right that a rogue stallion is trouble. If he continues to linger near the herd meadow, he will have to be driven away. A wild stallion cannot be tamed—he will never give up his freedom. He will only endanger our herd, just as you say. He will steal away mares to build his own herd. Our guards will be extra vigilant."

Toe-ta glanced up at the sky. The sun was an orange ball settling on the horizon. "As for Spotted Star, it is too late to search for her now. But try not to worry,

Sister. She may have wandered off and will return on her own. She can't be far. If she is still missing in the morning, our men will search for her."

Toe-ta turned Runner's head toward camp. "Let's go back," he told everyone. He raised his arm and the riders fell in behind him.

Kaya cast one last look at the woods. There was no sign of Ghost in those dark shadows. Speaking Rain took hold of Kaya's dress as they left the herd clearing and walked down the path toward camp, following behind the searchers.

They hadn't gone far before Kaya felt Speaking Rain's hand on her back. "Wait," her sister whispered.

When the sound of the searchers' footsteps had faded, Speaking Rain burst out, "Kaya, Ghost will never come back if he is driven away. And he *was* tamed, once. How else would he have gotten those whip wounds? I *know* he can be tamed again."

A twinge of uneasiness pulsed through Kaya. After all, when they'd seen Ghost earlier in the afternoon, he *had* been nosing at Spotted Star, right near the edge of the woods. Despite what Toe-ta had said, *could* Ghost have stolen Tall Branch's mare—or used his powerful medicine to draw her away?

"Maybe we should tell Toe-ta what we know," Kaya suggested.

"No!" Speaking Rain's eyes widened. "Not yet. I'm not ready to share our secret. Ghost needs to get more used to people. He isn't wild, but he would *act* wild if Toe-ta tried to catch him now."

"Aa-heh, I think you are right," Kaya said slowly. Anyway, even Toe-ta had said it didn't look as if Spotted Star had been stolen by a rogue stallion. And she couldn't betray Speaking Rain. With an effort, Kaya pushed her worries aside.

"Kaya, listen." Speaking Rain spoke urgently. "We have to try to tame Ghost as quickly as possible. If we can show he can be ridden, then Toe-ta will see how valuable he can be. It's the only way to prove he isn't really wild. I want to try riding him."

"Riding him? Speaking Rain, we don't know what kind of mount he is," Kaya pointed out. "He might have been ridden before, but that person beat him! How do you know he'll trust you to sit on him?"

"I don't," Speaking Rain said simply. "But I had my dream again last night. And this time it was *Ghost* I was riding. I knew him like my own brother. I trusted him and he trusted me. And Kaya—this is the *only way*. If he'll let anyone ride on his back, it will be me."

Kaya looked into her sister's face and read the urgency there. She swallowed and nodded. Then they hurried down the path toward the tepees.

Back at the camp, Eetsa and Kautsa set about preparing a meal of boiled salmon and mashed camas roots. Kaya helped them, and Speaking Rain sat with Wing Feather and Sparrow, telling them a story. Toe-ta sat nearby, mending a rope while the food cooked. Kaya tried to work extra hard, mashing the camas roots very fine and fetching water and the cooking stones for Eetsa. The big black hole in Tall Branch's sleeping furs loomed in her mind, mixed up with everything else that had happened that long day— Ghost's form in the woods, Tall Branch's face when she learned Spotted Star was missing, Speaking Rain's fears for Ghost.

Gradually, the familiar tasks of dropping the hot stones in the cooking basket and stirring the chunks of salmon soothed Kaya's frayed nerves. She relaxed and smiled at Kautsa for what felt like the first time that day.

But Tall Branch did not seem at peace. She was walking agitatedly back and forth among the tepees, twisting her hands in front of her. She paused and for an instant, her face sagged. Was that sadness? Kaya's heart twisted as she thought of how she'd feel if it were Steps High who had disappeared.

But in a moment, her aunt's face hardened again, setting itself in harsh, angry lines. She began glancing angrily at Kaya. Then she stopped and stood before the fire with her hands on her hips.

Kaya looked up from her stirring, startled at the figure looming over her. Tall Branch bent down and stared into Kaya's face as if searching for something there. Then her eyes narrowed and she straightened up. "The Stick People can be drawn by carelessness. And this girl is careless," she declared. "If that stallion didn't steal Spotted Star, then the Stick People must have taken her. And Kaya has drawn their notice to us."

Her words fell on Kaya like stones plunking into a pool. Kaya sat open-mouthed, staring at Tall Branch, who remained before her, head flung back, hands clenched into fists at her sides.

She had drawn the Stick People's attention? The Stick People were strong and clever, and they did like to play tricks. They sometimes even stole babies. They could steal a horse. And what they stole, they did not give back. And she *had* burned Tall Branch's furs. Had the Stick People noticed her careless mistake, as Tall Branch said? Kaya's palms suddenly grew sweaty. *No, she thought. That can't be right. Can it?*

Kaya looked from Speaking Rain, who sat straight up, listening hard, to Eetsa and Kautsa, kneeling with their hands idle in their laps.

Eetsa put her hand out to Tall Branch. "Sister, let us not speak hastily. These are serious words." Her forehead was creased with worry.

Tall Branch didn't even glance at her sister. No one else said anything. No one said a word in Kaya's defense.

The silence stretched out. Kaya couldn't stand it one more minute. She jumped to her feet. She didn't know what to do or what to say. She only knew she had to get away from Tall Branch and from the awful, doubting gazes of her family.

"I—I'll get more water," she said and blundered blindly from the camp. A few steps down the path, she heard Speaking Rain call, "Wait!"

She turned around and let her sister catch up. Wordlessly, they continued toward a brushy area where they'd recently been gathering sticks. Speaking Rain held Kaya's dress as she usually did, but this time, her grip seemed to be guiding Kaya rather than the other way around.

Once they were out of sight of the tepees, Speaking Rain stopped. She put her hands gently on either side of Kaya's face. "I can feel how upset you are, Sister." Her low voice was soothing. Kaya wanted to pull it over herself like a blanket. She wanted to shut out the awful turn this day had taken. "Tall Branch seems determined to point you out as a careless girl."

"I know." Kaya fought to keep her voice under control. She had done something dangerously careless once, when she'd lost Wing Feather and Sparrow when she was supposed to be watching them. For a long time after that, the other children had called her "Magpie," a selfish bird that thinks only of itself. She'd worked so hard these last three years to shed that nickname. And now she was being accused of carelessness again!

"Oh, Speaking Rain, what if Tall Branch is right?" Kaya whispered. Her throat ached so much that she could hardly get the words out.

"There is only one way to show everyone she isn't." Speaking Rain's voice was so firm that Kaya blinked and looked at her sister more carefully. She'd never heard her sound so confident, not even when she'd told the family she wanted to live with the Salish part of the year. "We must find Spotted Star ourselves. We can relieve Tall Branch's pain, *and* prove that the horse has not been stolen by the Stick People."

"Find her ourselves?" Kaya pondered her sister's words. "The men will be looking for her in the morning. They're experienced trackers. What can we do that they can't?"

"I've been thinking that Spotted Star might be with Ghost even if he *didn't* steal her," Speaking Rain said. "Remember yesterday afternoon, when Ghost was nosing around near Spotted Star? He's interested in her, and she's not adjusted to the new herd yet. Maybe she was lonely and wandered off with him. We can go search for her deep in the woods. The men won't think to look for her there—they'll be searching the open grasslands. And Ghost will let us approach him, but he'd run from the men." Her cheeks were flushed, and Kaya heard the urgency in her voice.

"That's a good idea—we'll search the forest first thing tomorrow. But..." A lump rose in Kaya's throat. "What if I *was* so careless that I drew the Stick People to us? I could never forgive myself. What if we never find Spotted Star? That will prove the Stick People have taken her forever."

Speaking Rain leaned forward. "Kaya, I believe in you. Not everyone does. But when Spotted Star is found—even if someone else finds her—they will all see the truth." She stood very straight, her braids blowing in the breeze.

Kaya felt as if she'd never really seen Speaking Rain before. Her sister looked so different all of a sudden, so tall and strong. Kaya had always been the one rescuing and taking care of Speaking Rain. But now her sister was taking care of her. And it felt good.

As if on an impulse, Speaking Rain put her hands behind her neck and untied a leather thong that held a single copper bead. She held it out to Kaya. "I want you to have this, Sister."

Kaya stared at the necklace. "But White Braids gave you this when you were rescued from the raiders!"

Speaking Rain nodded. "Aa-heh. She told me that I should wear it to give me strength as I recovered from my capture. Copper is strong, yet beautiful, she said, just like me. And now I'm giving it to you—to give *you* strength. We'll work through this problem side by side." She tied the necklace around Kaya's neck.

Kaya fingered the bead. It was still warm from Speaking Rain's skin—as if her sister's courage was flowing into her.

chapter 9

A Baffling Clue

THE SUN WAS already hot the next morning, even before it rose above the distant hills. The summer grasses were drying golden-brown and the leaves were wilted on the last of the camas plants. The root digging was almost over, and the big roasting pits were smoking with coals. Now the women were digging the new pit.

Kaya dug hard, working next to Rabbit and keeping one eye on Tall Branch. She had been avoiding her aunt ever since yesterday's accusation. Spotted Star still had not returned, and the men had left at dawn to search for her. Tall Branch sat near Speaking Rain and Bear Blanket, scraping roots clean before they were placed in the pits. Kaya could tell that Speaking Rain, too, was keeping her head down and working fast.

Urgency bound Kaya's chest. They were stuck here digging when they should be searching for Spotted Star. How were they ever going to get to the woods to search for her while they were trapped here?

Speaking Rain felt the same way—Kaya could see it in how stiffly she sat, her shoulders tight. Kaya wanted to scream with impatience, but she didn't dare let even a bit of her feelings show on her face. Not with Tall Branch here. Her aunt glanced up toward the diggers at that moment, and Kaya clenched her teeth and kept digging. She would never give Tall Branch a reason to accuse her of shirking work again.

At last, Eetsa sat back on her heels. "The pit is deep enough," she said, wiping her hand across her forehead. Her face was coated with dust and sweat. "We can smooth it out now and line it with rocks."

As the other women stood up and headed to the river to wash their hands and faces, Kaya shot to her feet. This was their chance.

"Speaking Rain and I can go get rocks. We can go to

the stony place back in the woods," she said, trying to keep the urgency from her voice. The stony place was near where Ghost liked to stay—and possibly where Spotted Star was too.

Eetsa nodded. "Take the travois and Brown Deer's old mare. She is tethered near camp, and she will be steadier with the heavy load than your Steps High. She is also big enough to carry you both, so you and Speaking Rain can ride double."

Kaya jumped to her feet and grabbed Speaking Rain. "Come on! Here's our chance!" she whispered to her sister. They hurried back toward camp.

"Don't forget grooming tools!" Speaking Rain called as Kaya stepped into their tepee and began throwing supplies for Ghost into a basket.

"I've got brushes and a comb," Kaya replied, ignoring the sweat that ran down her face. "And pemmican to feed him." She stepped out and let Speaking Rain heft the basket to feel how heavy it was.

"And here's the travois," Kaya said, lifting the

big stretcher made of two long poles with deer hide stretched between them. She led Brown Deer's big mare over to it and positioned her between the long sticks that protruded from the ends. Then she lashed the sticks to the harness she'd slipped over the mare's chest and shoulders. When the mare walked, she dragged the travois behind her.

They rode out of the camp and toward the herd meadow. "The searchers are fanned out across the prairie," Kaya told Speaking Rain, who was sitting behind her. Kaya leaned forward in her stirrups. "They must not have found her, because I can tell they're still looking."

"Good!" Speaking Rain said. "We'll have the woods to ourselves. They'll never think to go there—as we said yesterday, any lost horse would flee across open grassland, not into the woods."

"*Unless* she was lonely and following a handsome stallion," Kaya said. "Here's our plan: Let's get the rocks first. We can't shirk our work, not even now.

Then we'll look for Spotted Star, all around the place where Ghost usually is."

"And then we have to work on taming Ghost," Speaking Rain said. "We've *got* to do all this, Kaya— it's our only hope to find the mare *and* get back your good name."

"Then come on!" Kaya said, pressing her heels into the mare's sides. "Let's go!"

Once in the woods, they found the rocky place where many large and small stones lay tumbled about or piled up on each other. Working quickly, Kaya handed stones to Speaking Rain, who loaded them onto the travois.

When the travois was heaped with rocks, Kaya guided the horse to drag it under a tree. Then she untethered the mare and tied her near a patch of grass. "Now, let's look for any sign of Spotted Star," she said.

The clearing where Ghost liked to stay was deserted now, and the stallion was nowhere to be seen. Kaya bent to the ground, running her eyes over the leafy, muddy surface. She saw plenty of big prints from Ghost, but no smaller prints. Kaya moved back and forth around the clearing, gaze fixed on the ground. At the edge of the clearing, Speaking Rain stood perfectly still, her cloudy eyes unseeing but her whole body tense. Kaya knew she was listening for any sound of the mare—Speaking Rain's ears were as sharp as the best trackers' eyes.

"Anything?" Speaking Rain asked, when Kaya finally sighed and sat down on a big rock.

"Nothing," Kaya said. "No hoofprints, no white horsehair in the tree bark."

"And I haven't heard any sounds in the distance," Speaking Rain said. "I have to say it—I don't think Spotted Star is here."

"I don't either!" Kaya almost wailed. "Oh, Speaking Rain, what are we going to do? I thought for sure we'd at least find *some* sign of her!"

Speaking Rain put her hand over Kaya's. Her warm touch seeped into Kaya's skin, calming her.

"I thought Ghost would be here, at least," Speaking Rain said after a moment. "Where is he?" She raised her fingers to her lips and let out a long, low whistle, once and then again. Before Kaya could ask what she was doing, Ghost's silver-and-black form appeared among the trees.

"He came to your whistle!" Kaya exclaimed as Ghost ambled over to them. "But what's he doing coming from that direction?"

"I don't know." A big smile spread across Speaking Rain's face. "But I thought he might come to me." She put her arms around the stallion's neck. "You know us now, don't you?"

"He knows *you*," Kaya corrected. "He came to your whistle." She grinned as her sister flushed and stroked Ghost's neck. It wasn't often that she saw Speaking Rain acknowledge that she had done something special.

The horse allowed the hug but stood rigidly, quivering. His legs and belly were streaked with mud, and his coat was damp and sweaty. He snorted and threw his head in the air.

"Careful," Kaya warned. "He seems skittish to me. I don't think you should try sitting on him today. He's not calm."

Speaking Rain stroked the stallion's neck, then sighed. "Ah-heh, you're probably right. But Kaya, I *will* ride him soon. That's the only way to show Toe-ta that he can be tamed and find a place in the herd."

Kaya swallowed. "Yes," she said softly, but she could tell that her voice lacked conviction. "Quickly, let's feed him and get him clean. They'll be looking for us back at camp."

Speaking Rain opened the bag of pemmican, which Ghost inhaled almost without chewing. They brushed him from top to bottom. His back and shoulders were still badly scarred from the whip, but the open wounds were healing.

"What's this, Ghost?" Speaking Rain asked. She pulled something from the underside of his belly. "It feels like some kind of seed."

Kaya leaned over. Speaking Rain held several small brown seeds in one hand and ran her fingers over them. "I've never felt any like this before," she said. "They were clinging to his belly. Do you recognize them, Kaya?"

Kaya examined the seeds. They were long and thin and covered with small brown hooks. "I've never seen seeds like this. Strange—I thought we knew all the plants in this area. These seeds weren't in his coat last time we groomed him. Do you think he's been some-place new?"

"The seeds could be some kind of clue," Speaking Rain said. "If Spotted Star *is* nearby, maybe these seeds could help tell us where."

"I don't know," Kaya said doubtfully. "There's no sign of her around here at all. And look at Ghost. He's with *us*. If he were guarding a mare, he'd be with her." She handed the seeds back to Speaking Rain. "Here, put them in your pouch. Maybe someone can tell us where they're from."

Speaking Rain folded the seeds into a little square of soft deerskin and placed them in her waist pouch. Then the girls harnessed Brown Deer's horse to the travois and rode out of the woods, into the herd clearing. The herd horses were standing nose to tail, their ears relaxed, dozing in the warm sun, tails swishing flies.

As they rode past the herd, Toe-ta came toward them on Runner, the horse's powerful chest pushing through the tall grasses. "I've come to help you with the travois, girls. We were not able to find the mare in this morning's search."

A pang of worry struck Kaya at the news that Spotted Star was still missing. But she was careful to keep her face untroubled. "Katsee-yow-yow for helping us, Toe-ta," she said. She helped him move the travois to Runner, letting Brown Deer's mare rest from the heavy load. Just as Toe-ta was about to fasten the travois, Ghost suddenly slipped through the trees, close by the herd. Kaya caught her breath.

"Ah, there is the stallion we saw yesterday," Toe-ta

said with interest. He mounted Runner and sat quietly, watching Ghost. The girls watched, too.

Ghost stepped delicately from the trees and eyed another stallion in the herd, a young horse named White Face. White Face lifted his nose, scenting the strange stallion, and flattened his ears. Ghost walked deliberately over to a clump of grass near White Face and dropped his head, nibbling. But there was tension in his body, Kaya could see, and she held her breath, waiting.

Ghost took a step closer to White Face, goading him. White Face flattened his ears, but before he could move, Ghost spun and kicked out at the young stallion with violent force. Kaya gasped when she saw the small bleeding wound on White Face's rump. The young stallion screamed with rage and danced, ears pinned, trying to bite Ghost's neck. But the older stallion easily evaded the swipe and reared up, meeting White Face in the air, and for a long moment, the two stallions pawed the air with their hooves and manes flying, the powerful muscles in their haunches gleaming and bulging.

"That's enough!" Toe-ta roared and squeezed Runner into a gallop. He raced the bay through the fighting horses, knocking them both off balance. White Face dropped down and trotted to the edge of the herd. Ghost wheeled and without a backward glance galloped into the woods, his silver tail flying behind him.

Kaya breathed a sigh of relief, but Toe-ta shook his head. "That stallion is up to no good," he said. "We cannot have a wild horse harassing our own stallions." Toe-ta deftly fastened the travois, remounted Runner, and led the girls toward camp.

"Maybe the stallion is just seeking a place in the herd," Kaya said tentatively to Toe-ta's straight back.

"No." Toe-ta's single word cut through Kaya like a knife. "Wild stallions can never be tamed. They can never accept the ways of people over the freedom they've had," he said. The peaks of the tepees were in sight now. "If he keeps staying close to the herd, we will have to drive him away. We can't have anything endanger our horses. They are too important to us."

"But . . . what—what if the stallion was *once* tamed?" Speaking Rain said from her place behind Kaya. Kaya could tell she was trying to speak carefully, so as not to give away their secret or displease their father even more. "Could he find a place in a herd then?"

Toe-ta's face was set as if carved from wood as he guided Runner. "Once a horse becomes wild, he can never go back, no matter his past," he said. "We know this from our many years with horses as our brothers. That horse must be run off."

"Oh, please, Toe-ta, don't drive him away just yet!" Speaking Rain burst out. "Let's give him a chance."

Toe-ta glanced at Speaking Rain over his shoulder and his face softened. Kaya knew that Toe-ta especially liked to grant Speaking Rain's requests.

"We will wait a short time, Daughter," Toe-ta conceded. "Perhaps the stallion will leave on his own."

Kaya looked over her shoulder. Speaking Rain's face was full of worry. The time for them to prove that Ghost could be tamed was growing very short.

Later that afternoon, Kaya knelt at the edge of the new roasting pit, carefully fitting the rocks they had gathered against the smooth dirt sides. Though her hands moved constantly, Kaya did not see her work. Instead, she pictured her sister's worried face as she'd spoken with Toe-ta. Kaya knew how much Speaking Rain wanted Ghost to stay with their herd. But could he be tamed again? And even if he could, would they have enough time to do it? Training horses was a slow, patient process—not something to be done under pressure. And what about Spotted Star? They hadn't found her in the woods, and the men hadn't found her on the prairie—so where could she be?

She's with the Stick People, of course, a little voice said in Kaya's head. She shoved the voice away. And what about the strange seeds stuck in Ghost's coat? What did those mean?

Her mind swam. She kept seeing Tall Branch's angry face before her eyes, her pointing finger as she declared, "If that stallion didn't steal Spotted Star, then the Stick People must have taken her. And Kaya has drawn their notice to us."

I have been careless recently, Kaya thought miserably. *I've been so eager to get out and find Ghost. What if Tall Branch is right? What if it's my fault her beautiful mare is gone, stolen by the Stick People?* She swallowed hard and pressed her fingers around Speaking Rain's copper bead at her throat.

"Kaya!" Eetsa called. "Leave the roasting pit, and come help prepare the evening meal."

Kaya got to her feet and returned to the camp. Eetsa and Speaking Rain were kneeling by the fire outside their tepee. Speaking Rain was stirring cooking stones in a basket. Eetsa pulled them out with two sticks, one by one. Toe-ta sat nearby, waiting for his meal.

"And we will be back before sundown," Toe-ta was saying to Eetsa.

"Where are you going, Toe-ta?" Kaya asked as she piled newly roasted camas roots into bowls. Eetsa ladled out the freshly cooked salmon.

"Jumps Back and I have decided to ride to your aunt's village, to see if her mare has run back to her home herd. The journey will take most of a day—we will leave after the morning meal tomorrow."

At her father's words, relief rushed through Kaya. Of course—a lonely horse would run back to her home village! Kaya allowed herself to feel the tiniest glimmer of hope that Spotted Star wasn't with the Stick People after all. But how was she going to wait all day to hear the news from Tall Branch's camp? Kaya wished she could ride out there right now, by herself, galloping Steps High all the way.

Eetsa handed Kaya a wooden bowl of steaming fish. "Bring this to Tall Branch," her mother said. "She is not feeling well and is resting on her sleeping mat."

Kaya took a deep breath. Maybe this was a chance to help make up to Tall Branch for being careless. Whether she *had* drawn the Stick People's notice or not, burning Tall Branch's furs was inexcusable. She could arrange the meal perfectly, to please her. Tall Branch liked things pretty and neat, Kaya could tell.

Carefully, she arranged the camas roots in Tall Branch's bowl so they were stacked tidily. She tucked the family's best carved spoon beside it. The bowl of salmon was steaming hot and smelled delicious. But there had to be something more. Kaya looked around the pile of baskets that held their foodstuffs. Her eye fell on a little bag of dried huckleberries they'd gathered last year. Their supply was almost exhausted since this year's berries were not quite ripe yet. Surely the last of the huckleberries would please Tall Branch.

Kaya tipped the jewel-like fruits into a pretty bowl made from a piece of horn. Eetsa had traded for it with one of her partners from the east. Tall Branch might never have seen something like that before.

Balancing the bowls of camas and berries and leaving the salmon behind for a moment, Kaya tiptoed to the tepee entrance and quietly lifted the flap. Tall Branch was sitting with her back to Kaya, her head bowed, rocking back and forth a little. She was making a small choking, sniffling sound.

"Aunt?" Kaya said timidly.

Tall Branch twisted around in surprise. She was holding a folded bit of deerskin in her hand. A few dried leaves were piled in the middle. Her face was wet with tears.

Kaya stood at the doorway, the bowls of food in her hands, not knowing what to do. Tall Branch saw her and wrapped the deerskin shut, laying it by her side. She turned away and swiped the tears from her cheeks.

"What is it you want?" she demanded. Her clipped voice sounded the same as it always did.

Kaya stepped forward, extending the bowls. "I brought you your meal. With the last of the huckleberries," she added. She tried to smile.

Tall Branch raked the bowls with a critical eye. "No fish?"

"I have it right here." Kaya stepped back outside to fetch the salmon. She arranged the bowls in front of Tall Branch and handed her the carved spoon. "Toe-ta carved this spoon himself," she pointed out. She sat back on her heels and watched Tall Branch's face.

Tall Branch picked the spoon up and tasted a huckleberry. "Sour," she pronounced.

Kaya's shoulders sagged.

"But katsee-yow-yow just the same," she said, taking another bite. She offered a small, tight smile and nodded toward the tepee flap, dismissing Kaya.

Tall Branch had thanked her! Kaya could hardly believe she'd heard it. But why was her aunt crying over some dried leaves?

Kaya slipped from the tent. Eetsa and Speaking Rain were eating their own bowls of salmon, kneeling on mats near the fire. Kaya sat down quietly beside her sister.

"Did your aunt like her meal?" Eetsa asked, taking small bites of the steaming fish.

Kaya ladled out her own bowl. "I—actually, I don't know," she confessed. "She thanked me, but she seems very sad." She leaned close to Eetsa and Speaking Rain. "She was crying over some dried leaves."

Eetsa set down her bowl and sighed. "I'm afraid you're right. Tall Branch is very sad. You know that her husband died and that is why she came to live with us."

"I know," Kaya nodded.

"Well, those leaves are a special tea that her husband would gather for her. It's a tea that only their band collects, and I believe it is not easy to find. Tall Branch loved that tea. She would always serve it to me when I visited her. And now it must be almost gone— her last reminder of the husband she loved." Eetsa shook her head and picked up her bowl again.

Speaking Rain's brow was creased, but she was quiet, eating her fish.

"Oh, that's so sad," Kaya almost whispered. She thought of how her heart had been wrenched when her mentor, Swan Circling, had died one terrible winter. At least she had Swan Circling's saddle. Using it always made her feel as if her mentor's spirit was with her. But to have only a bit of tea—Kaya's eyes were pricked by unexpected tears. At last, she knew what Tall Branch might be feeling.

And maybe, Kaya thought, sitting straight suddenly, there might be a way to help her—and to search for Spotted Star at the same time. She felt Speaking Rain's hand squeeze her own. Kaya squeezed back. She knew her sister was thinking the same thing.

Toe-ta rose. "Katsee-yow-yow for the meal," he said to Eetsa. He set his bowl down and strode off toward the path to the herd meadow.

Kaya and Speaking Rain set down their bowls and ran after him. "May Speaking Rain and I go with you tomorrow when you ride to Tall Branch's camp?" Kaya asked.

Toe-ta looked surprised. "It will be a hard day's ride."

"We won't slow you down," Kaya promised. "We want to see if we can get more of Tall Branch's tea for her—to help her feel better." She did not mention that they also wanted to see with their own eyes whether the mare had returned to her old home—without waiting all day to hear the news.

The lines in Toe-ta's face split into a smile. "Aa-heh, that is thoughtful of you, Daughter. You and your sister may come along."

Kaya exhaled a deep sigh of relief. Speaking Rain leaned against her back for a moment, as if a weight had been briefly lifted from her shoulders.

chapter 10

A Turn for the Worse

KAYA THOUGHT SHE'D never lived through such an endless night. The need to get back to the woods so that Speaking Rain might try riding Ghost ate at her like a gnawing hunger. But Eetsa and Kautsa had kept her working until almost bedtime to finish the roasting pit.

When pink morning dawned, Kaya opened her eyes and felt the urgency pull at her. They would leave after the morning meal to ride to Tall Branch's village. She must help Speaking Rain ride Ghost this morning—it was their last chance.

The icy water of the river splashed Kaya's face as she and Speaking Rain bathed with the other girls. "Come on," Kaya said quietly as they dried themselves on the riverbank. "Eetsa won't need us for a little bit. We can slip out to the woods now."

"Yes," Speaking Rain said, her face alive. "I'm ready! Let's find Ghost."

Holding hands, they trotted up the path from the river and skirted the edge of the village. They broke into a run once they were out of sight, bounding through the herd meadow and into the woods.

They found Ghost grazing peacefully in his usual spot. He raised his head at their approach, his jaws moving lazily.

Speaking Rain exhaled as she ran her hands over his ribs. "See, Kaya, how he's a little fatter? Already I can barely feel his ribs."

"His coat is shinier too," Kaya told her. "It's like the light at dawn reflecting off a lake."

Speaking Rain was humming a low tune in her throat, running her hands all along Ghost's neck and shoulders, down his back to his powerful flanks. "I had my dream again last night. I was riding Ghost. I knew him like my own brother." She smiled at Kaya.

Kaya tried to smile back, but she couldn't help noticing how small and delicate her sister looked, standing beside the massive stallion. *If he hurts her . . .*

"Please just be careful," Kaya begged. "He's not even wearing a halter."

"Oh, I will." Speaking Rain's voice was tranquil. "Let me tell Ghost what we're thinking of." She leaned over and murmured to the horse, patting his back several times. Then she looked back at Kaya. "All right. I'm ready."

Speaking Rain grasped the thick mane in both hands. Kaya saw Ghost tense. He lifted his head and swiveled his ears back to catch what Speaking Rain was doing, then sidestepped a little as if trying to evade the grasp on his mane.

Speaking Rain lifted her foot so that Kaya could leg her up.

Kaya grasped her sister near the knee and lifted. Speaking Rain flung her leg over the broad barrel and pulled with her hands. Breathless, she sat up straight.

Ghost gave out a little nicker and danced to the side. His head was very high, his neck pulled back, all his muscles bunched. Suddenly his tail lifted and his head went down. "Watch out, he's going to buck!" Kaya warned.

Speaking Rain could read the signs as well as Kaya could, Kaya knew. She too had ridden since her hands were big enough to hold reins. She gripped with her legs, her hands high on the horse's neck. "Easy there, easy," she crooned.

Ghost dropped his head and gave a little buck, which Speaking Rain sat, and then began trotting in a fast, small circle, shaking his head.

Kaya's stomach felt as if it were filled with a hundred grass snakes. "Slide off, he's not safe," she called.

"I can do this!" Speaking Rain said, her voice strained and breathless. "I just need him to calm—" Her weight slipped a little to the side, and the horse exploded like a pine knot in a fire.

He gave a tremendous buck, head down, heels

kicking high in the air, then bucked again and again. Speaking Rain was being thrown around like a rag doll, and before Kaya could make a move to do—*what,* she didn't know—her sister was tossed to the ground in a heap.

Kaya ran to drag her out of the way of the dangerously plunging hooves, but Speaking Rain was already crawling forward. Ghost wheeled and galloped back into the trees, leaving nothing behind but hoofprints—and heartbreak.

Speaking Rain pushed herself slowly to sitting. She buried her face in her hands.

"Are you hurt, Sister?" Kaya gasped, kneeling beside her.

Speaking Rain did not answer. Her shoulders heaved up and down.

"Shall I run back for Bear Blanket?" Kaya shook her shoulder gently. "Please, talk to me!"

Her sister slowly raised her head from her hands and Kaya inhaled sharply. Blood trickled from

Speaking Rain's nose, pooling on her upper lip, and a bloody gash was slashed across her cheek. Through the mud and blood, tears coursed down her cheeks, making two clean tracks.

"I'm not badly hurt. Just shaken. But—oh, Kaya, he threw me!" She choked on the words, and Kaya flung her arms around her sister.

"What if I never ride him?" Speaking Rain went on. "What if my dream meant nothing? What if he really is too wild, as Toe-ta said? Kaya, they'll drive him away!"

"He just wasn't ready! That's all. We need to practice with him more." Kaya tried to believe her own words.

Speaking Rain didn't answer. She climbed stiffly to her feet, her hand pressed to her hip. "We need to go back," she said dully. All of the spark had gone out of her face. "Toe-ta will be wanting to leave soon."

Kaya swallowed. "Aa-heh," she whispered. They started from the clearing.

Speaking Rain's voice came from behind her, hard and clear. "It was a foolish dream. I'll never ride him."

They walked out of the clearing and back to camp.

"Speaking Rain!" Kautsa gasped when they walked up to the tepee. They were late. The others were already sitting at their morning meal. "You're hurt. What has happened to you?" She set her bowl on the mat and climbed to her feet. Gently, her strong, wrinkled fingers touched the dried blood crusting Speaking Rain's face.

"I wasn't paying attention and—and I fell," Speaking Rain said.

Kaya could tell by the firm tone of her sister's voice that she didn't want Kaya to say anything.

"Kaya!" Kautsa rounded on her other granddaughter. "Where were you? Why did you let your sister get injured?"

"I—I . . ." Kaya's stomach twisted as she tried to

think of what to say. Speaking Rain did not want her
to tell about Ghost yet.

"Kaya was nearby," Speaking Rain cut in. "But she
couldn't reach me in time."

"That was foolish," Tall Branch's voice rang from
near the tepee wall. She sat bundled in her deerskin,
though the morning was already warm. "And Kaya,
you should have taken better care of your sister.
Carelessness—again."

"I—" Kaya began. But what was she going to say?
She felt Eetsa's soft hand on her back.

"Fetch water and a washing cloth," her mother
told her. "I will make a salve for your sister's cuts."
She sighed. "Kaya, Tall Branch and Kautsa are right.
You should be watching your sister more carefully.
I fear you are sliding back into the carelessness we all
thought you had outgrown."

*I **am** watching Speaking Rain!* Kaya seethed as she
hurried away for water. No one knew the truth! But
as she dipped a small bowlful of water from the big

basket, the flames of her anger died down. What Eetsa
had said was true in a way. She had not safeguarded
Speaking Rain enough—and now the rest of her family was agreeing with Tall Branch that she was careless.
How long until they also believed that she had brought
the Stick People's notice to them? How long until they
also blamed her for Spotted Star's disappearance?

Kaya clenched her jaw. *Speaking Rain is right that she
will never ride Ghost,* she told herself. *Because I will not
let her put herself in danger again.*

With Speaking Rain's face cleaned and a quick bowl
of camas mash in their stomachs, Kaya and Speaking
Rain followed Toe-ta and Jumps Back from the camp
a short time later. The sun was still low in the eastern
sky. Steps High's familiar rhythm was soothing, but
Kaya's thoughts churned like salmon at spawning time.
Just behind her, Speaking Rain rode quietly on her gray
mare. Kaya clutched her sister's lead rein tightly. She
wasn't going to be blamed for any more mishaps.

"Kaya," Speaking Rain said once, softly.

"Shh," Kaya replied. "We'll talk later."

"I was just going to say that I hope Spotted Star is at the village. For Tall Branch's sake and yours."

I do too, Kaya thought, a bit grimly.

chapter 11

Tall Branch's Village

KAYA AND SPEAKING RAIN rode in silence, with only the squeaks of the wooden saddles and the clop of the horses' hooves to break the quiet. Kaya followed Jumps Back's powerful shoulders and the haunches of his black mare. Ahead, she could just see Runner's bay form, with Toe-ta astride.

Kaya thought miserably of how excited and hopeful she'd felt yesterday when Toe-ta had announced the visit to the village—how she'd imagined finding Spotted Star, returning her to Tall Branch, and clearing her name. Now, even if they did find the mare, Kaya would still be in disgrace for carelessness. She felt the sudden prickle of angry tears and blinked them back hard. In trying to help Speaking Rain save Ghost, she'd only brought trouble on them both.

This is our last idea to find Spotted Star, Kaya thought. *If she isn't at the village, there's nowhere left to look. If we don't find her today, I might as well just accept it: The Stick People took her, and it's my fault she's gone.*

"We will stop here." Toe-ta's deep voice came back to them. He drew rein, and the others halted beside him.

In front of them spread open land as far as they could see. The rocky soil had disappeared, giving way to soft mud that oozed up over the horses' hooves. In the distance, small trees spread out like dark smudges on the horizon. Nearby, grassy hummocks sprouted tufted heads of yellow-green grass. Patches of water glinted gray under the sky, broken up by soft hillocks of turf and low brown and green plants.

Suddenly Kaya realized where they were—the bog! She moved closer to Toe-ta.

"Tall Branch's village is on the other side, beyond those trees," Toe-ta said. "But the bog is large, and we cannot ride through it. The danger of quicksand is too great. We must ride around it."

Kaya thought of the last time she had seen the bog.
She and Raven and Fox Tail had ventured out to the
edge of the woods last year and gazed at the bog from
the shelter of the trees. The bog's thick, peaty odor
had surrounded them. From somewhere in its midst,
a small animal had screamed as it met its death in the
talons of a hawk.

"Spirits live there," Raven had whispered, and the
horses had slung their heads about, trying to turn back
toward camp.

Now Toe-ta led them along the edge of the bog. As
if the miasma of the place had permeated her mind,
Ghost and his unearthly ways floated through Kaya's
thoughts. Like the bog, he too was mysterious. With
a sinking heart, Kaya realized that their troubles had
begun right after he appeared: Tall Branch's accusations,
Spotted Star's disappearance, her own carelessness.
Did Ghost have some sort of strange power? Something
passed down from his ancestors, the Ghost Wind
Stallions? *Maybe he's using his powers for harm, not good,*

whispered a small voice at the edges of her mind.

After some time, Toe-ta guided the riders away from the bog and onto the higher prairie. Kaya shook her head and forced the disturbing thoughts away. She had to focus on finding Spotted Star. That's all she could do right now to make things better—and Tall Branch's village was just ahead.

At the top of a rise, Kaya could see the village of long reed-covered structures below—the longhouses that Tall Branch's band lived in all year round. Curling around the village was the silver snake of the river. It was odd to see longhouses in harvesttime, instead of tepees. Kaya's band put up longhouses only in the winter. Kaya leaned forward in her saddle and squinted. A smattering of brown, white, and black forms was scattered outside the village.

"I see the horses!" Kaya whispered to her sister.

"Do you see Spotted Star?" Speaking Rain asked.

Kaya squinted and rose in her stirrups. There were white horses, but none with the special bright white of

Spotted Star. "I don't see her yet. But that doesn't mean she's not there." Kaya tried not to betray the sliver of doubt that poked at her.

They rode down the hill, the horses leaning back on their haunches against the slope. Kaya couldn't see the herd anymore, with the horses now hidden behind the longhouses. She longed to ride straight out to them and search for Spotted Star, asking everyone along the way if they'd seen her. But Toe-ta and Jumps Back rode straight toward the village. Kaya knew that it was only proper to greet the elders first.

As they neared the longhouses, groups of children ran out to welcome them. The riders dismounted and handed their horses to two little girls. Two women and a man were walking toward them, their hands outstretched.

"Welcome," said the man. He looked older than Toe-ta, and his braids were streaked with gray. "We are pleased to see cousins from the prairie. I am Beaver Tail."

Toe-ta stepped forward. "Katsee-yow-yow for your welcome. We have come with a reason." Quickly, he explained Spotted Star's disappearance.

Beaver Tail frowned. "We know that horse well. If she had returned to our herd, we would have sent a messenger to return her."

Kaya's shoulders sagged. Speaking Rain sighed.

"But perhaps our hunters have noticed signs of the mare," Beaver Tail went on. "Come with me. We will ask them."

He led Toe-ta and Jumps Back away. Kaya wanted desperately to go with them, but one of the women smiled warmly at Speaking Rain and Kaya. "You are tired and hungry, young travelers," she said. "I am Red Stone. Please come and have a meal." Kaya knew they could not refuse her invitation without offending Tall Branch's people.

The girls followed the women to some tule mats on the ground near the entrance to the longhouse. The children crowded around them, staring curiously.

Women sat in groups, weaving or making rope together. A young woman named Two Crows, who looked about Brown Deer's age, poured cups of water. Kaya and Speaking Rain drank gratefully. Red Stone put a bowl in front of each of them with mashed fish and kouse finger cakes.

"Now," she said, settling herself on her knees and picking up a partially woven basket. "How is our cousin who came to you not long ago?"

Kaya stared in the direction Toe-ta had gone. Perhaps at this moment, he was hearing news of Spotted Star. He had to be! This was their last chance to find her. She realized the women were watching her and forced her mind back to the conversation. "She misses her mare—we had hoped that Spotted Star would be here."

Two Crows shook her head. "Ah, I wish she were. Tall Branch loves that mare very much. She raised her from a foal."

Kaya swallowed. For the hundredth time, she

hoped with all her heart that she wasn't the cause of Spotted Star's disappearance.

Speaking Rain spoke up. "There is another reason for our visit. We wanted to see if you had some of the tea Tall Branch likes so much—the tea her husband used to make for her."

Kaya leaned forward and held her breath. If they didn't bring back Spotted Star, maybe at least they could bring back the tea to comfort her aunt.

But the women were already shaking their heads. "Ah, sadly, no. We don't have any more just now. The tea is brewed from a plant that grows in boggy places. We have only recently settled here. We haven't yet explored the bog nearby to replenish our supply."

A pang of disappointment pierced Kaya's chest. Were they going to fail in both their goals?

"We rode past the bog on our journey, but our band does not go there," Speaking Rain said.

Red Stone rose to her feet and picked up Kaya's and Speaking Rain's empty bowls. "Your people are right to be cautious. Bogs are dangerous. But we river people know bogs well. Many plants grow there that grow nowhere else. The plant that Tall Branch's tea is made from, for instance." Red Stone described the small plant with its distinctive purple leaves. "Many bog plants have leaves and seeds that aren't like those of other plants," she added.

Speaking Rain opened her pouch and pulled out the long, thin, hooked seeds they had plucked from Ghost. "Do you know these? We found them recently, and we don't know what plant they come from."

Red Stone bent close to Speaking Rain's palm while Two Crows looked over her shoulder. "Aa-heh, these seeds are from a bog plant we know well," Red Stone said with surprise. "This plant grows only in bogs. I thought you said you didn't go there."

From a bog plant. Ghost had seeds stuck in his coat from a bog plant. Which meant . . . he'd been to the bog where none of her people ventured. What was he doing there? What did he want in the bog? Kaya's stomach grew heavy. Whatever Ghost wanted in the bog couldn't be good.

"Now, Tall Branch's husband," Red Stone went on, *"he* would have been the one to ask about the seeds. He knew more than anyone else in our band about plants and seeds. That's how he knew about the plant for tea."

Kaya turned her thoughts back from Ghost and Spotted Star. She asked a question she'd been wondering about since Tall Branch arrived: "How did he die?"

"It was a terrible accident," Two Crows sighed. "He was out hunting deer and was struck by one of our men's arrows."

"Tall Branch cared for him during his long sickness afterward," Red Stone said. "Through all the season of the deep snow, she watched over him. The healers said they could not help him, that he would die, but she would not leave him, even for meals. We brought her food to his bedside. In the season of melting snow, he died. We thought our tribeswoman might die as well. She would not eat, would not come out of her longhouse."

"We feared for our village," Two Crows told them. "Tall Branch was one of our leaders. We relied on her strength to help us through the deep winter."

"She was suffering..." Speaking Rain said softly, and Kaya felt a wave of sympathy for Tall Branch. It was hard to imagine her as a grieving widow, or a brave, trusted leader. Still, it was true. Maybe...maybe Tall Branch had reasons for being so angry and harsh.

Speaking Rain touched Kaya's hand, and Kaya knew that she was thinking the same thing. For the first time that day, she felt that her sister's mind was joined with her own once more.

As they rode away from the village a short time later, Kaya could hardly contain her impatience to talk to Toe-ta. His face and Jumps Back's had betrayed nothing when they returned to the longhouses.

"Toe-ta, the women have seen no sign of Spotted Star," she said softly to her father's broad back.

"And the hunters we spoke with have not seen the mare either, nor any sign of her," Jumps Back replied, twisting around in his saddle. He gave Kaya a sympathetic look.

Kaya looked down at her pommel as the men rode ahead. She rarely cried, but the crushing despair that descended on her seemed to force the tears to her eyes. Angrily, she rubbed away the drop that fell on the worn leather.

"We didn't even get the tea," Kaya burst out. "We went all this way and didn't accomplish either of our goals. We'll never get Spotted Star back." She glanced at the clean but still angry-looking gash on Speaking Rain's cheek and felt the weight pressing on her even more heavily when she thought about having been accused of carelessness again that morning, in front of everyone.

Maybe Tall Branch had been right about her all

along, Kaya thought miserably. She had drawn the Stick People with her carelessness. It was her fault Spotted Star was gone. After all, the mare seemed to have vanished without a trace, just as if the Stick People really had taken her.

And then, had she made another terrible mistake by helping Speaking Rain try to tame Ghost—this strange horse who showed up out of nowhere and brought odd dreams and powerful medicine with him? She should have been *protecting* her sister from this horse when in fact, she'd been doing just the opposite. A little groan escaped Kaya's throat.

Speaking Rain must have heard her, because she leaned forward from her position just behind Kaya. "Don't give up, Sister. We'll keep looking for Spotted Star. I just *know* we'll find her. And Kaya—I was thinking about Ghost bucking me off this morning. I should have listened to you: He just wasn't ready. And we've been taught that Nimíipuu never give up. So I'll try again tomorrow, with your help, and—"

"No, you won't!" Kaya burst out.

Speaking Rain started in surprise. Kaya panted, trying to still her suddenly racing heart. But the anger inside her still bubbled like a cooking basket full of hot stones.

"I'm sorry." Kaya spoke carefully. "I don't think you should try to ride Ghost anymore. You could get hurt again. And they'll all accuse me of not protecting you." Kaya knew her voice sounded measured and cold. She couldn't help it. It was the only way she had of not crying anymore.

"But Kaya..." Speaking Rain fell silent. Kaya could tell she was too shocked to say more.

Kaya carried the lump in her throat all through their silent ride back. Everything was a mess—and she'd made it that way.

Journey to the Bog

chapter 12

"KAUTSA, I'M TROUBLED in my mind,"
Kaya said.

The riders had returned at dusk from their trip to
the village. Speaking Rain had mumbled that she was
tired and had ducked into the tepee to sleep, but Kaya
was restless. Sleep was the last thing she wanted. Now
the evening was turning to night, and Kaya sat in front
of Kautsa near the tepee as her grandmother combed
out her braids.

"Hmm," Kautsa murmured. "Your hair is rough,
Kaya. You must put bear grease in it every night to
keep it smooth and shiny."

Despair washed over Kaya. They hadn't found
Spotted Star. Speaking Rain wanted to ride Ghost
again—and Kaya still did not know if he meant harm

or not. She felt she could not carry the unbearable weight any longer. All she could see was Speaking Rain, tumbling from Ghost.

"I'm troubled that Tall Branch is right," Kaya said, low. It was hard to say the words, but she made herself.

"Ah," Kautsa said, pulling the comb through the tangles. "You are worried that your carelessness did attract the Stick People, who then stole Spotted Star. And I know you are troubled by your sister's injuries and the further accusations this morning."

"Aa-heh," Kaya said. She tried to swallow the huge lump that had risen up in her throat. She didn't dare speak of her suspicions about Ghost. She couldn't ruin Speaking Rain's dream. And yet the horse could be out to harm them. It would be such a relief to unburden herself to Kautsa. Kaya bit her lip, so that the pain would remind her to hold back her words.

Kautsa was quiet for a long moment, smoothing her hand down Kaya's long river of hair. Kaya closed her eyes. It felt good to sit with her grandmother after all the tension of the last few days. The evening air was soft and scented with smoke from the roasting pits, which smoldered night and day.

"You know that you were careless, burning Tall Branch's furs by accident," Kautsa said. "That is what upset your aunt at first. And we depend on you to be your sister's protector." *You did not do that.* The unspoken words floated in the air.

Kaya bent her head, accepting the sting of the words.

"But I also know you have worked hard to shed the nickname Magpie, given to you when you were younger," her grandmother went on. "Now it's time for you to work to prove that you are not a careless girl. How you will do that is up to you." She finishing plaiting Kaya's hair again, two shiny ropes as strong as the ones that Speaking Rain wove.

It's up to you. Kautsa's words spun through Kaya's mind as she lay next to Speaking Rain in their furs that night, the quiet breathing of her family all around her. After a long time, she fell asleep, her mind still troubled.

But when Kaya opened her eyes the next morning, she knew what she wanted to do—at least part of it. Maybe she couldn't save Spotted Star *or* Ghost, but she could try to make amends with Tall Branch. She could do that.

Kaya took a deep breath and spoke words she never thought she'd hear herself say. "Speaking Rain," she whispered, nudging her sister. "I want to go out to the bog. I want to gather some of the tea plant for our aunt." She would take the tea to Tall Branch. And maybe by thinking carefully of what could help Tall Branch, she would counteract her carelessness from before. If the Stick People *had* stolen Spotted Star, just maybe they would even bring the mare back.

What Kaya would do to make up for not protecting Speaking Rain, she didn't know yet.

Outside, the morning sky hung flat and white. Wisps of mist curled among the tepees and clung to Kaya's bare arms. She shivered as she and Speaking Rain hurried down the path to find Eetsa.

Their mother was filling a water basket at the edge of the river. She listened to the girls' request and nodded her head. "Aa-heh, you may go to the bog, but do not ride into it—the bog can be dangerous. If you don't find the plant near the edge, you must leave without it."

Kaya swallowed hard. She fought the urge to turn and run down the path, back to the tepee and away from spooky bogs and ghostly horses. "We will!" she promised her mother.

As soon as they had bathed and eaten, Kaya and Speaking Rain went to the herd meadow. They caught their horses, mounted, and rode out of camp, following the path they'd taken with Toe-ta, breathing in the mellow scent of the morning air.

Kaya's heart pounded as they neared the bog. The air was very quiet. There was no breeze to ruffle the leaves or cool the sweat on their necks.

"This is it," Kaya said when they reached the bog. It spread before them, brooding to itself under its layer of mist.

Her sister nodded. "I can feel how soft the ground has become. We'd better not go any farther. The bog must be right in front us."

"Yes," Kaya said. "Here, we'll just ride along the edge, the way Toe-ta and Eetsa told us."

Kaya looked carefully for the plant with the distinctive purple leaves that Red Stone had described. Kaya and Speaking Rain had ridden only a short distance when Kaya spotted it. "There, Speaking Rain!"

She climbed down from Steps High and plucked the leaves from three plants, being careful not to disturb the roots. She placed them in her waist pouch and then pulled out a few dried berries to give to the Stick People. She usually left this gift when she gathered food, as did all the Nimíipuu, but this time, her hand paused as she placed the berries on a leaf. "Please," she whispered to the air. "Please accept the gift as a sign of my respect for you." She'd never spoken to the Stick People before, but if they were listening, she wanted them to know that she was aware of their power—now more than ever.

"Let's go," Speaking Rain said, lifting her face to the breeze. "The bog is making me shiver."

"Aa-heh," Kaya agreed. "It's a strange spot, isn't it? Not like the rest of the land." She put her foot into her stirrup, grasping Steps High's mane and preparing to mount, when something silvery caught her eye. When she bent closer, she saw that it was a tuft of long hair caught in the grasses and fluttering. Kaya picked up the hair and examined it. "Speaking Rain, how odd. A clump of hair—horse-tail hairs, I think." She handed a strand to her sister, who rolled it between her fingers.

"It has the same texture as Ghost's," Speaking Rain said. Kaya once more marveled at her sister's sense of touch. All horsehair felt the same to her.

"It's the same color, too," Kaya told her. "A bright, bright silver, like a lake in the morning."

"Ghost's hair . . ." Speaking Rain suddenly put her hand in her waist pouch and pulled out the little hooked seeds. "Red Stone told us these seeds we found on Ghost come from a plant that grows only in bogs."

"Ghost *must* have been here in the bog," Kaya said, puzzled. "But why would he come out here? It's not good grazing land. The grass is much better out on the prairie." She tried not to let her worries about Ghost's nature show in her voice.

"I don't know." Speaking Rain shook her head slowly. "Kaya, I've been thinking a lot about Ghost. I want to apologize for asking you to help me ride him again. I'd never want you to be accused of not protecting me—you *do* protect me, all the time. I—I won't ask you again."

Good! Kaya almost shouted. *He's dangerous!* But then she looked at her sister's face, full of sad resignation. Suddenly, she knew. She knew what she could do to make up to Speaking Rain. Kaya pushed her worry away. She'd do anything for Speaking Rain. She would do this.

"Speaking Rain, you came out to this place today to help *me* make amends to Tall Branch," Kaya said slowly. "You gave me the copper bead that White

Braids had given to you, to give me strength after
Tall Branch accused me. You've thrown yourself into
finding Spotted Star. And why have you done all this?
Just to help me. You give me so much. And I know
that riding Ghost, proving to Toe-ta that Ghost can be
tamed, is what *you* want—so that you can fulfill your
dream. My sister, I'm going to help you ride him. As
you said yesterday, he just wasn't ready yet when you
tried before."

Speaking Rain looked astounded. "But—but Kaya,
what if I get hurt again? You'll be blamed for that."

For the hundredth time, Kaya pushed back her
fears about Ghost. "I have to protect your spirit, too,
don't I? Bear Blanket always says the body is just a
container for the spirit. If I protected your body but
hurt your spirit, I think the Stick People would be
offended by that too!"

chapter 13

An Offering for
Tall Branch

KAYA FOUND HER aunt bent over the camas
roasting pits when they returned. She was taking the
night's covering of branches off the smoldering pits to
check the roots. All around, other women were remov-
ing roasted roots, adding fresh ones, peeling the last of
the newly dug roots, and placing the cooked roots in
baskets to be brought to camp.

The flowers were wilted and the camas field was a
maze of crushed plants and digging holes. The root harvest was almost over. Many other bands of Nimíipuu
were already packing their tepees and gathering their
horses for the trek into the foothills for berry picking.
Kaya's band would soon follow, splitting in two, with
the women and children picking berries, while most of
the men and older boys went out to hunt.

Kaya took a deep breath. "Aunt?" she said.

Tall Branch straightened up and turned around. "Yes?" Her face was unsmiling, but her voice was not harsh.

Kaya resisted the urge to back away. She made herself say the words she had planned. "Will you go with me back to the camp? I—I have a surprise for you there."

Tall Branch's eyebrows drew together, but after a pause, she followed Kaya back to the tepee. Speaking Rain was there, as they had planned, and Kaya knelt beside her. Tall Branch knelt also and looked around.

"I'm not fond of surprises," she said sharply. "There is plenty of work to do at the roasting pits."

Silently, Speaking Rain handed Kaya a cup of the steaming tea they'd prepared earlier. Kaya just hoped they'd brewed it correctly. She held it out to Tall Branch.

Her aunt took the cup and smelled it. She looked up, pure happiness and surprise spreading over her face. "My favorite tea!" she exclaimed. "Where did you find it?"

Kaya and Speaking Rain grinned at each other. "We hope you like it," Kaya said.

Tall Branch took a sip and then another. Her face softened. "It is perfect," she almost whispered. She stared into the cup as if seeing a landscape in its amber liquid. Speaking Rain quietly picked up a rope she was weaving and began twisting the strands.

"Kaya," Tall Branch said suddenly. "It was very kind of you and your sister to find this tea for me." She seemed to be forcing her words out as if they did not come easily. "I know I have been hard on you since my arrival here."

Kaya glanced at Speaking Rain, but her sister was focusing studiously on her rope. Tall Branch took another long sip of tea, and then, as if the brew had given her strength, she set the cup down firmly. "It's time for me to explain. My husband was a great hunter and warrior, but sometimes, he led with his heart instead of his head. His greatest fault was that he sometimes acted before he thought, leading to careless mistakes."

Kaya swallowed. She thought of that long-ago day when she had raced Steps High with her cousins instead of watching her brothers. The twins had nearly been lost, and that's when she had been given the nickname Magpie. "I understand." She nodded.

"My husband went on a deer hunt with the other men of our village," Tall Branch went on, gazing across the camp at the pine trees in the distance. "A magnificent buck ran into arrow range. One of the hunters shouted that he had the shot. But the others told me that my husband did not think. He rushed forward to shoot the buck himself—and ran right into the other hunter's arrow. It hit him in the abdomen. That is how he died."

The words seemed wrenched from Tall Branch's lips. Kaya remembered Red Stone telling them of the long months Tall Branch had spent caring for her husband after that day, never leaving his side. She wanted to reach out and take her aunt's hand, but she sat quietly instead.

Tall Branch looked again into her cup and swirled the tea there. "Now I cannot bear to see others making careless mistakes. When I do see carelessness, I am harsher than I would like to be." Her eyes when she looked up were pleading. "Please see that I was only trying to help you, Kaya. Perhaps not in the best way."

Kaya let out a breath she didn't realize she'd been holding. Speaking Rain squeezed her hand. "Katsee-yow-yow, Tall Branch," Kaya said simply. "I have been careless. Katsee-yow-yow for watching over me."

For the first time since Tall Branch's arrival, she smiled at Kaya. Kaya smiled back, feeling as if a load of firewood had been slipped from her shoulders.

"Now," Tall Branch said, settling herself more comfortably and sipping her tea again. "Tell me how you found this tea. What a surprise this is!"

Kaya and Speaking Rain told Tall Branch of their

visit to her camp and their journey to the bog.

"Ah, the bog!" Tall Branch nodded. "I know bogs well. Whenever we found one, we would collect seeds and berries there. Plants grow in bogs that grow nowhere else. Bogs have many gifts." Tall Branch's face was animated. Kaya had never noticed before how her dark eyes sparkled. The bog has gifts! She'd never thought of it that way before.

Tall Branch went on. "Of course, we have to be vigilant. The bogs can also conceal traps."

"Traps?" Speaking Rain asked.

"Aa-heh. Bogs have patches of quicksand that can catch a person and hold them fast—or even swallow them up," Tall Branch said. "Our band has ways of telling where the quicksand lies and how to avoid it, but people who don't know bogs have been caught in them over the years."

Tall Branch laid a hand on Kaya's knee. "Kaya, I know I have accused you of something serious— of causing the disappearance of Spotted Star. No one can know the ways of the Stick People, not even me. But let me say now that I hope I was wrong."

"I do too," Kaya said softly.

Tall Branch sighed. "More and more, I think it was that stallion who stole my mare. Your father says he's still around the herd. That stallion is a menace."

Her words punched into Kaya like a fist. She didn't have to look at Speaking Rain to know that her sister felt the same. Kaya had made amends with Tall Branch—but what would happen to Ghost?

chapter 14
Speaking Rain's Sacrifice

LATER THAT DAY, Kaya mounted Steps High and waited for Speaking Rain to swing up onto the gray mare. They were going to look for Ghost. The time had come for Speaking Rain to try again. Kaya's heart felt torn in two. This might be Speaking Rain's only chance to ride her Ghost. He might be gone soon. Spotted Star was gone; Speaking Rain's dream must not be lost as well. *I can't do much for her,* Kaya told herself fiercely. *But I can do this.* No matter what happened, she and her sister would be one again.

"This time I'll start slower," Speaking Rain said as she rode just a few inches behind Kaya. "I won't actually sit on him until he shows us he's ready."

"Aa-heh, I hope he will." *Because this could be our last time.* Kaya didn't have to say the words. Speaking

Rain knew it as well as she did.

A few more minutes of hard riding brought them to the rocky area where they usually found Ghost. Kaya looked around. "I don't see him. Ghost!"

Speaking Rain put her fingers to her mouth and whistled. Almost immediately, they heard an answering whicker, somewhere to their right.

They found the stallion in a small meadow, standing hock deep in grass, like a silver spirit in the midst of the brown and green. He raised his head and whickered again when he saw them, then cantered over. Kaya caught her breath all over again at his beauty. Maybe her worries were wrong. Maybe he was just a horse.

They dismounted and tied their horses to a nearby shrub. Then the girls stood silently, side by side, gazing at the stallion. He looked back at them with his huge, dark eyes.

"Ghost, we are here." Speaking Rain's simple words fell like drops of rain in the silence of the meadow.

She began to stroke him all over, and he stretched his neck and half-closed his eyes with pleasure. Speaking Rain spoke softly to him. "We want to help you. Please let us show Toe-ta you can be tamed. Please let me sit on you." She placed her left hand on Ghost's neck and he turned his head to snuffle her hair. Delicately, he nibbled her shoulder with his sensitive lips. Speaking Rain giggled and kissed his muzzle. Then she turned to Kaya and took a deep breath.

"Ready?" Kaya asked. She tried not to let her anxiety show in her voice.

Speaking Rain nodded. She stood close to Ghost's side, at his shoulder, and gripped his mane near the withers, her right hand on his back, applying gentle pressure. Then she waited. Kaya knew her sister was trying to sense the tension in the stallion. Kaya watched him closely. He raised his head at her touch and flicked his ears, but he did not pin them back. This time, Speaking Rain did not move again until she felt Ghost relax his head and neck. Kaya knew that meant that he had decided to accept her grip.

Then Speaking Rain raised her left leg. Kaya took Speaking Rain's knee in both hands and lifted Speaking Rain lightly onto Ghost's back. Every muscle in Speaking Rain's body was alert, Kaya could tell. Kaya fixed her eyes on Ghost, watching him for any sign of an explosion. He stood with his ears swiveled back, sensing Speaking Rain.

Speaking Rain slowly stroked Ghost's neck. Kaya did not breathe.

Then Ghost bobbed his head up and down. He shifted his weight and swiveled his ears forward and back again. Kaya exhaled. He was signaling that he was going to allow Speaking Rain on his back. Kaya closed her eyes. Tears prickled under her eyelids.

Speaking Rain, sitting tall and relaxed, stroked the long scars that ran over Ghost's withers. Her sensitive fingertips grazed the rough surfaces. Kaya couldn't help thinking of the last time the stallion had likely had someone on his back. It was almost certainly the person who had given him those scars.

Speaking Rain reached down and stroked Ghost's neck. "No one is holding you," she murmured. "No one is making you carry me. You've decided. Katsee-yow-yow, my beautiful horse."

Speaking Rain made no attempt to move Ghost with her legs or seat. She just sat easily, patting and talking to him. After a few moments, he dropped his head, his muscles relaxed, and he lifted his nose to nibble a few blades of grass.

Speaking Rain sighed a deep sigh of contentment. She gave Ghost's neck a final pat, and slid down. Her face was split in a grin bigger than any Kaya had seen.

Kaya grinned back. "You did it, Sister. You rode your horse." They swung onto their horses and started from the meadow. Ghost ambled away from them, shaking his head against a few flies, heading to a soft patch of grass.

"Far from it," Speaking Rain corrected her. "I *sat* on

my horse. Riding will be something entirely different."
But the grin stayed on her face as if glued there.

"Still, you might be able to ride him," Kaya said.
"And that *might* be enough to show Toe-ta he can be
tamed."

"Aa-heh," Speaking Rain admitted. "But we have
a long way to go."

A noise from behind them made Kaya turn around.
Ghost was still standing in the meadow, but two mares
had emerged from the trees to join him.

"Oh no!" Kaya gasped, her hand going to her
mouth.

"What?" Speaking Rain asked. "What is it?"

"He's taken two mares." Kaya felt sick just saying
the words. "Brown Deer's old horse and that black
mare that Jumps Back rides. He's cut them away from
the herd and he's hidden them back here." As if to
confirm her words, the black mare wandered toward
the edge of the clearing and Ghost swiftly trotted after
her, lowering his head almost to the ground, pinning

his ears back, and deftly turning her back into the meadow. The message was clear: These are my mares now, and they're staying with me.

"Do you see Spotted Star?" Speaking Rain sounded as if she could barely force her voice to work.

"No," Kaya told her. "She's nowhere to be seen."

"But if he's been stealing mares, just as Tall Branch suspected, then—"

"He's endangering the herd." Kaya swallowed. "Just as Toe-ta said he might. He must have been too weak before, but now, with our feeding him and helping his wounds to heal, he has more strength..." All the good feelings of a few moments before evaporated in her like water sizzling on a hot stone.

Speaking Rain swallowed hard and patted the top of Ghost's head. The stallion had returned to their group and was standing close to her and her horse. "Of course, Spotted Star's not here..." She trailed off, but Kaya didn't have to say what they both knew. It meant nothing that Spotted Star wasn't in the meadow.

It didn't change the fact that Ghost was now a threat to the herd, even if he did let Speaking Rain ride him.

Speaking Rain slipped off her horse and put her arms around Ghost's neck. She leaned her head against his warm coat and stayed there for a long time. Kaya saw her shoulders lift and fall once and knew her sister was trying not to cry. Kaya sat silently on Steps High, biting back her own tears.

Finally, Speaking Rain turned away from Ghost. She closed her eyes and seemed to shrink down into herself, but then she straightened her back. "Now we must go to tell the others. Right away." She swung back onto the gray mare. "They need to know that Ghost is endangering the herd. We must set aside our love for him—for the good of us all." She sat very tall in the saddle and her words were strong and clear.

Kaya looked into her sister's face and thought she'd never seen such bravery as the bravery she saw there.

...

A short time later, Kaya and Speaking Rain sat silently together near the tepee. Wing Feather and Sparrow hopped about nearby, but the girls paid them no attention. It was all over. They had told Toe-ta and the others what they knew about Ghost. They'd told Toe-ta what they'd found in the meadow. Everyone agreed that Ghost could no longer be allowed to linger near the herd. They were now preparing to drive him off—permanently.

Speaking Rain's face was pale and her mouth was set in a straight line. Kaya patted her back but didn't dare to do more. She knew it was taking all her sister's strength to keep from breaking down. Kaya tried to shut her ears to the sounds of the preparations—the clinking of the tack as the horses were saddled, the low talking of the men, the occasional snort from the mounts. She glanced over quickly and saw Toe-ta quietly slip a quiver of arrows into his saddlebag.

She didn't look anymore after that.

"We are ready to go!" Toe-ta shouted. The band

was mounted, standing ready, with weapons on their backs or saddles. Kautsa laid a hand on Kaya's shoulder. Kaya averted her eyes from the riders. She clasped both of Speaking Rain's hands in hers as the sound of pounding hooves faded away.

chapter 15

A Slender Hope

KAYA COULD HARDLY bear the oppressive quiet that hung over the camp after the riders left. All she could picture was Ghost, so beautiful, being hunted, wounded by arrows and driven away with shouting and blows with a whip. She saw his dark eyes widening in surprise, his whinny of fear as the riders descended on him, shouting—

"Kaya." A hand landed on her shoulder. She jumped. Tall Branch was standing over her.

"Can you and Speaking Rain help me sort some of my things?" she asked. "They've been in such a jumble since I arrived."

With a twinge of surprise, Kaya managed a smile as she followed her aunt and her sister to the tepee. Was it possible that Tall Branch was trying to help them

174

by giving them a task to distract them?

The dusky, cool interior of the tepee seemed a world removed from the bright chaos outside. Speaking Rain and Kaya knelt beside Tall Branch, folding the mats and ropes she handed them, placing leather thongs into different baskets.

"Here, would you sort this basket of Spotted Star's gear?" Tall Branch handed them a large basket brimming with horse items: bridles with rope bits, brushes and combs, little pouches of salve for wounds. Speaking Rain began separating the brushes while Kaya folded the rope bits. They worked mechanically, not speaking, for a few minutes. Then Speaking Rain froze. Her fingers held a clump of white mane or tail hairs. She must have just plucked them from the brush in her lap.

"What is it?" Kaya asked.

Her sister rolled the hairs between her fingers. "These hairs—they're Spotted Star's?" she asked Tall Branch.

"Aa-heh," Tall Branch replied, looking puzzled. "I use these tools only on her. In fact, I groomed her with that brush the last time I rode her, just before she disappeared."

"Tall Branch!" Kautsa's voice called from outside. "Will you come and give your opinion on this last batch of roasted camas roots? We are just taking it from the pit."

Tall Branch climbed to her feet. "Don't worry too much about your stallion, girls. I'm sure he will find his way to another herd. And perhaps Spotted Star will come back to us after all." The tepee brightened momentarily as she lifted the flap.

The moment the flap closed, Speaking Rain grasped Kaya's arm in a grip so tight it almost hurt. "These hairs! They're Spotted Star's—but Kaya, they feel just like the ones we picked up at the edge of the bog." She dug into her waist pouch and pulled out the tuft of long silvery horsehair they'd found in the grass of the bog.

"You mean Ghost's hair?" Kaya asked.

"That's just it!" Speaking Rain pulled a single hair from the tuft and laid it on the tule mat. Then she laid one of the hairs from Spotted Star's brush beside it. She ran her fingers over both. "They feel exactly the same. Are they the same color?"

"Aa-heh," Kaya said. "They are!" She lifted the door flap to let in more light. The hairs glinted side by side on the mat, the exact same shade of silvery white. The same shade as Ghost's tail—and the same shade, Kaya suddenly realized, as Spotted Star's tail. "Speaking Rain!" she gasped. "The hair we found in the bog—it wasn't Ghost's hair, was it? It was Spotted Star's! And that means—"

"Spotted Star must be in the bog," Speaking Rain finished. "She must have tried to return home, as we first thought. Going through the bog would be the shortest route back to the village—but also the most dangerous. And we know she did not make it home." Speaking Rain jumped to her feet. "Come on. We must get help. Spotted Star has been gone so long already. We may not have much time left to find her alive."

Kaya's chest was tight and her breath came fast as they ran from the tepee down the path to the roasting pits. The bog could swallow people. It could swallow horses. Spotted Star could be trapped there—or dead. She tripped and Speaking Rain stumbled into her, but they both scrambled up and kept running. Kaya barely noticed the blood trickling down her scraped knee.

"Eetsa! Tall Branch!" Kaya called as they neared the pits, panting. But the pits were deserted. Wildly, she looked about, Speaking Rain close by her side. "They're not here—where are they?" Then she saw that the pits had been emptied. The women must have taken the roots away from the roasting area to be ground.

"We can't take time to look for the women—and we don't know where the men are now either. They could be anywhere, looking for Ghost." Speaking Rain grabbed Kaya's arm. "We must go to the bog ourselves. If Spotted Star is in trouble, we have to find her."

Together, they ran for their horses, tethered with a few others near the camp. Flinging their saddles on their mounts' backs, they swung into the seats. Kaya clapped her heels to Steps High's sides. Just as the horse leaped forward, Speaking Rain shouted, "Wait!"

Kaya reined Steps High back. "What is it?"

Speaking Rain slid off the gray mare and found her way to a pile of horse gear nearby. She ran her hands over the pile and pulled out two thick coils of rope. Kaya caught the one she tossed over. "We'll take the fastest path to the bog!" she shouted to Speaking Rain. "Through the herd meadow and into the woods!" If they followed that path straight through the belt of woods, it would lead them to the open prairie on the other side—and on to the bog.

Looping the ropes over their pommels, they galloped together toward the meadow.

chapter 16

A Desperate Ride

"GO THROUGH THE woods," Kaya panted as they neared the main horse herd. Steps High's hooves pounded beneath her and she crouched low over her horse's neck, the wind whipping her face. Just behind Steps High, Speaking Rain galloped the gray mare on her leading rein.

Kaya wheeled Steps High onto the woods path. Tree branches whipped her face, and she slowed Steps High to a lope and bent her head to keep clear. Through the branches, she could faintly hear the men's voices as they searched, but the sound receded quickly.

The woods closed in around Kaya and Speaking Rain. As they rode deeper, the thick forest canopy made a false twilight. Suddenly, in the gloom, a flash of silver darted through the trees. "Ghost!" Kaya reined

Steps High in. "Speaking Rain, I saw him!"

Speaking Rain wasted no time, but brought her fingers to her lips and whistled low and clear. Instantly, Ghost's familiar form appeared among the brush. "He's hiding from the searchers back here," Speaking Rain breathed as she rode over to him. She bent down. "I'm here, friend." She stroked his ears. "It's time for us to say good-bye." Her voice caught. "It's—it's my fault, Ghost. I'm sorry. You're not safe. And we must go to the bog. Spotted Star is there—we think."

The girls put their heels to their mounts and followed at a fast lope through the winding tree trunks. "We can't hide Ghost from Toe-ta and the others," Kaya called softly as they ran, "but if he's running on his own, we don't have to stop him."

The woods thinned and prairie opened up before them. Steps High galloped on steadily, and Kaya silently thanked her for being such a reliable mount. Ghost was still with them. He ran just ahead of Speaking Rain as if he were her protector.

"He's taking us to the bog," Kaya suddenly realized. "He's leading us there." Why? Was he leading them into a trap? Or did he know something they only suspected—that Spotted Star was trapped there?

The bog suddenly spread before them—dank, marshy, thick with the rank odor of the peat. Kaya reined Steps High in, and Speaking Rain, a few steps behind, heard her movement and pulled the gray mare up too. The three horses and two riders stood alert at the edge of the soft ground. Kaya's eyes scanned the landscape, searching for any sign of the horse. Speaking Rain sat straight and silent. Kaya knew she was listening for movements or whinnies.

The moments ticked by. A cloud passed across the sun, throwing the landscape into darkness, and then light spilled over them again. The wind rustled the bog grass. Far away a crow cawed. But there was no sign of Spotted Star.

"Ghost!" Kaya yelled in frustration. "Where is she? Why did you lead us here?" She smacked her hand on the pommel of her saddle.

The stallion just looked at her with his fine dark eyes and dropped his head to nibble a tuft of dead grass. Kaya slumped in her saddle. It was all for nothing. They'd risked the elders' anger for nothing. Kaya's name could not be cleared now. Tall Branch's grief could not be relieved.

Kaya turned Steps High back toward the woods. "We might as well go home," she said, trying to sound calm. She had to be strong, after all, for Speaking Rain's sake. "We can tell Tall Branch that we tried at least."

She heard a little intake of breath behind her. It sounded like Speaking Rain crying. Well, that was to be expected. After all, her horse—and the horse she'd come to love—would soon be driven off forever.

Kaya swiped her hand under her eyes and turned Steps High again so that she could comfort her sister.

But Speaking Rain wasn't crying. She was sitting perfectly straight and her face was ablaze with color. Kaya blinked.

"Listen!" Speaking Rain held up her hand.

Kaya listened. The crow again, the wind. The creaking of their own saddles. Ghost crunching his grass.

"There!" Speaking Rain tensed. "I'm sure of it this time."

"What? What?" Kaya stopped herself from leaning over and shaking her sister, the suspense was so intense.

"Whinnying!" Speaking Rain burst out. "Far away and so faint, but a horse is out there in the bog! And we're going to find her!" She turned to Ghost. "You must not come with us, friend," she told him. "Wait here. We won't be long."

Then, giving the gray mare her head on a loose rein, Speaking Rain led the way into the treacherous bog.

Kaya's fingers were numb on the reins as she followed her sister. The ground was dangerously soft. Even if they didn't sink in quicksand or mud, either of the horses could turn an ankle in this footing. The black mud sucked at Steps High's feet and the mare shook her head and snorted nervously, her head up and her ears swiveling, ready to find any danger in this strange place.

The gray mare picked her way around the grass hummocks. Several times, Speaking Rain stopped to listen for the whinnying, and finally Kaya heard it too—a distant, frantic neighing. The sound jolted her insides with equal parts fear and joy. It must be Spotted Star—if only they could reach her in time!

Then Kaya saw her, hidden behind a clump of scrubby bushes and far from the edge of the bog. Kaya grasped the pommel of her saddle to keep from weeping with relief.

"I see her, Speaking Rain. I see her!" was all she could say. "Ghost led us to her! He must have tried to follow her when she ran from the herd. She must have been trying to get home. Cutting through the bog is the shortest way. And Ghost must have followed her—that's how he picked up the seeds on his belly."

A great wash of relief crashed over her. Ghost must be good. He must be—he had led them straight to

Spotted Star. He had tried to help them.

But Kaya's relief was short-lived. Spotted Star was stuck nearly up to her belly in thick black mud. Her body and face were splattered black. And she looked terribly weak. She kept resting her nose on the mud in front of her, where it would start to sink. Then she would pull it up again, but soon she was resting her head down again. Kaya could see that it wouldn't be long before she didn't have the strength to lift it at all. She would lay it down for the last time and let her mouth and nose sink into the mud that would suffocate her.

"Speaking Rain, we don't have much time." They slid off their horses and quickly tied them to a scrub bush. Kaya described the scene in detail to Speaking Rain as she led her sister closer to the mud pit. "She's weak now. I don't know how we're going to get her out, but she won't be able to help much. The mud pit is deep, but it's not much bigger than she is. The ground at the edge of the mud pit turns soft gradually." It was mucky and soft, like the rest of the bog, but it wasn't sinking at least.

Speaking Rain knelt and tested the ground with her hands, then crawled forward slowly, pressing the turf, until she reached the edge of the mud pit. Then she felt her way around the edges of the pit, reaching out now and then to touch Spotted Star. "She's very thin. She's had no food since she was trapped here. We'll never get her out unless she has something to eat. Luckily, she could reach that little puddle of water to drink. Otherwise, I'm sure she never would have lived this long."

"But how are we going to get her out?" Kaya asked. Panic was starting to rise up in her again. They didn't have long. Already, Spotted Star's eyes were glazing and she was resting her head in the mud for longer and longer times. It was clear that she would not live much longer. There was no time to ride back for help. If they were going to save this horse, they were going to do it now—by themselves.

Speaking Rain nodded and took a deep breath. "I have an idea. I don't know if it will work. But here—" She took a cake of pemmican from her pouch. The greasy, fatty mixture of camas flour, deer fat, and berries was good fuel for hunters. It would be good energy for Spotted Star, too—if she could eat it.

Speaking Rain handed the cakes to Kaya. Leaning precariously over the edge of the mud pit, Kaya held the cake out under the mare's nose. The horse snuffled it and then, with both girls holding their breath, lifted her lip to nibble a bit. Kaya exhaled. Spotted Star was eating.

When Spotted Star had eaten all the cake, Kaya climbed to her feet. "Now. Tell me your plan."

Speaking Rain nodded. "We are not strong enough to help Spotted Star from the pit by ourselves. But we have two horses, and we have ropes. We might be able to harness Spotted Star to Steps High like a travois. With you urging her on, Steps High could pull her forward. I'll go to Spotted Star's rear. I can shout at her and tap her rump with a branch to get her to move forward." Both girls knew that a horse would move away from pressure on its rump.

Kaya thought for a moment—but only a moment. "Let's try it." It was the only plan they had. They did not know yet if it was a good one.

They retrieved the long loops of strong hemp rope from their saddles and, working very carefully so that they didn't fall into the mud, they managed to pass double loops of rope across Spotted Star's withers and down behind her front legs, as if they were cinching on a saddle. Then they passed the rope loops up past her chest and laid them out flat on the solid ground near Steps High, who stood waiting. As they worked, Kaya gave silent thanks that Spotted Star was not stuck more deeply. If the mud had been up past her belly, they never would have been able to get the rope around her.

Spotted Star stood motionless as they worked. Her sides heaved in and out, but she didn't have the strength to struggle.

Kaya wiped her arm across her forehead. In spite

of the chill, she was sweating. Speaking Rain felt over the loops of rope, then nodded. "All right. Can you back Steps High near the loops?"

"Aa-heh." Kaya untied her horse and positioned her so that she was facing away from Spotted Star, with the rope loops on the ground on either side. Then, Kaya and Speaking Rain managed to run the loops through the girth on Steps High's saddle and pass them across her chest. That would let her pull forward with the power of her whole body, without yanking her saddle off.

"We're ready!" Speaking Rain said. "You work with Steps High and I'll encourage Spotted Star from the back. Get me a big stick."

Kaya broke a large branch off a nearby shrub and handed it to her sister, then smoothed her mare's sleek nose. "You need to help us, girl—Spotted Star needs you." Her heart was pounding in her chest, but she made sure Steps High saw only that she was calm and in charge.

"I'm ready!" Speaking Rain called. She was standing just at the edge of the mud pit, a little to the right of Spotted Star's tail. "Go!"

Kaya cried, "Forward, Steps High!" She slapped her mare on the rump and clucked, then twirled the end of the lead rope and caught Steps High just behind the girth. Steps High lunged into the rope harness. The ropes tightened. At the same time, Speaking Rain swung the branch against Spotted Star's rump with a *wump!* The horse jumped a little. "Go! Go!" Speaking Rain cried. She hit Spotted Star again. Steps High lowered her head and pulled. Suddenly there came the sucking sound of a massive vacuum breaking. A tremendous slurp erupted from the mud and Kaya dared a glance back over her shoulder. To her joy, she saw Spotted Star's chest emerging from the pit, her mud-blackened forelegs scrabbling for purchase.

"More, Steps High!" she yelled. *"Pull!"*

"Get up! Get up, girl!" Speaking Rain ran forward, tapping Spotted Star on the belly. The mare jumped in surprise, lurched forward. More sucking sounds emerged from the mud. Spotted Star's back legs pistoned powerfully and her flanks trembled with effort. Then, with a mighty heave, she flopped her front legs onto solid ground.

"You're almost there, girl!" Kaya shouted. "Come on!"

"She's doing it! She's doing it!" Speaking Rain screamed from behind.

With a painful scraping, inch by inch, Steps High dragged the down horse forward, Spotted Star's body stretched out grotesquely. Kaya held her breath. Spotted Star's back legs were still trapped. Her belly stretched along the ground. Steps High bent her head and Kaya gave her a hard slap on the rear. "Pull!" she shouted again, and with a slurping, sucking sound, Spotted Star's back legs emerged from the mud, paddling wildly. She flopped onto her side on the ground.

"She's out! We did it!" Speaking Rain yelled. She grabbed Kaya around the shoulders in a fierce hug.

Kaya hugged her sister back and closed her eyes in thanks.

But their work was not done. As quickly as she could, Kaya unharnessed Steps High. "Katsee-yow-yow, my horse." She ran her hand along her mare's sweaty back. "You have done good work today. You saved Spotted Star."

Speaking Rain was untying the ropes that wrapped Spotted Star. The mare was a pitiful sight, coated in black mud, her former beauty only a memory. But then she rolled onto her chest and pushed herself up on her forelegs. Speaking Rain, feeling the horse's movement, backed away. Kaya didn't breathe. Then, her back legs quivering with the tremedous effort, the mare heaved herself to her feet.

"She's up!" Kaya said.

Speaking Rain smiled. "And she'll live. Let's take her home."

chapter 17
Going Home

GHOST WAS WAITING for them at the edge
of the bog. He flicked his ears forward when he saw
them and touched noses with Spotted Star. A spasm
crossed Speaking Rain's face and she rested her head
on his neck.

Kaya stood beside her, her own throat aching. She
didn't say anything. There wasn't anything to say.

At last Speaking Rain raised her head. Her eyes
were shiny but her face was composed. "Your name
will be cleared now, Kaya," she said. "At least we have
that. And we'll have our memories of Ghost." Her
voice caught.

Something fierce welled up in Kaya. She shook
her head. "No!"

"What?" Speaking Rain asked, startled.

Kaya began to pace back and forth. "I said no. We're not going to let Ghost go without a fight. My name is cleared now, and Tall Branch's pain will be relieved soon. Now it's *your* turn."

Speaking Rain pushed herself away from the stallion. "Kaya, what are you talking about?"

"I'm saying we're going to show Toe-ta, Tall Branch—*everyone*—that Ghost can be tamed. He *can* be a part of our herd." Kaya clenched her hands into fists. "And if he's part of the herd, he won't need to cut away mares. He'll have all he wants, just like the other stallions."

"Kaya, it's too late," Speaking Rain said. "Toe-ta has made his decision."

"And I've made mine," Kaya insisted. "We're going to *show* them that Ghost can be tamed—that he *has* been tamed."

"How will we do that?" Speaking Rain asked faintly.

"We'll bring him home with us!" The words fairly

bubbled from Kaya's mouth. "When we bring Spotted Star. And then you will sit on him, right there in front of everyone."

Doubt struggled with hope on her sister's face. Kaya put her hands behind her neck and untied the thong that held the copper bead Speaking Rain had given her. Gently, she fastened it around her sister's throat. "You gave me this to give me strength through a hard time. Now it returns to you, to give you the strength you need."

Speaking Rain touched the bead. Kaya held her breath. Then a faint smile lifted the corners of Speaking Rain's mouth. "Let's try it, Sister," she said. "I'm ready."

Their progress back to the camp was slow. Spotted Star hobbled, terribly weak. Ghost followed them willingly, his head bobbing and his rich silver coat shining in the late-day sun. Kaya listened sharply for the sounds of the trackers, but she heard none. They must have given up the search, at least for now.

As they neared the herd meadow, Kaya imagined how they must look—two riders, mud-splattered and disheveled, emerging from the woods with a creature between them that no one would recognize—a sorry skeleton of a horse, so muddy that she looked black. And behind them, an apparition—all silver and black.

When they drew close to the circle of tepees, Kaya could see Toe-ta and the other hunters standing together in the camp. Tall Branch stood close by. Toe-ta was shaking his head. "We lost him," he was telling Tall Branch. "But we will resume our search tomorrow. We found the mares he'd cut away. They've been restored to the herd."

Just then, Spotted Star let out a high nicker at the sight of her owner. Every head turned toward Kaya and Speaking Rain. The mare broke into a stiff trot. Tall Branch uttered a cry and ran forward. Everyone stood at a respectful distance as Tall Branch bent her head into the neck of her mare. Kaya was fairly sure her tough aunt wouldn't want anyone to see her weeping.

Kaya and Speaking Rain walked slowly into camp, leading Ghost. Toe-ta stepped forward, his brows drawn together. His face looked cut from oak. Speaking Rain stopped in front of him. The stallion stood just behind her, his head over her shoulder.

"What is the meaning of this, Daughters? Where did you find Spotted Star? What do you mean to do, bringing this stallion into our camp?" His voice was deliberate and measured. He meant to be answered.

Silence blanketed the crowd. Speaking Rain's hand trembled on the lead rope. Kaya's heart pounded like a drum in her ears.

"I will tell you everything, Toe-ta," Speaking Rain said, her voice shaking. She steadied herself. "I will tell you all how we came to find Spotted Star, and why I brought this wild stallion to our camp."

With everyone sitting around the family's campfire,

Speaking Rain spoke for a long time, so long that
Yellow Flower went to her cooking fire and returned
with cups of tea for everyone. She was interrupted only
by the nearby crunch of Spotted Star eating from a pile
of grass that Tall Branch had brought her. Speaking
Rain told of her longing to ride alone. She talked of
how she and Kaya had discovered Ghost in the woods
and their friendship with him, and of her dream
about riding Ghost, even before she had met him. She
described the scars on his back and the loneliness that
had drawn him to the herd. She told of the seeds that
had led them to the bog and the silvery hairs that had
led them back. Of how desperate they were to find
Spotted Star, for both Tall Branch and Kaya. And how,
if Ghost had a place with their herd, he would no longer steal mares. He would have friends and mates, just
like the other stallions. She talked and talked, and by
the time she fell silent, the sun was sinking fast below
the tepees and shadows were creeping toward them,
long and chill.

Then Speaking Rain rose to her feet. "Our elders thought this horse, wild as he was, could never be tamed."

Kaya could hear how respectful her sister kept her voice. She knew that Speaking Rain would never want to contradict Toe-ta.

Her sister went on. "I want to show all of you that he can be tamed—he *has* been tamed. Kaya, would you help me?"

With her knees trembling and her mouth dry, Kaya stepped forward and stood beside Ghost as Speaking Rain picked up a bridle from a pile of tack nearby. She slipped the bridle over his head. He looked around alertly, his head high and his ears forward.

Please, Ghost, Kaya silently pleaded. *Your whole life is in the balance, right now. Please behave.*

Speaking Rain moved slowly and calmly, but Kaya, standing next to her, heard her sister's rapid breathing and saw the slight shaking of her hands as she stroked and murmured to Ghost.

"I'm ready, Kaya," Speaking Rain said, and Kaya legged her up onto Ghost's back as gently as she could.

Ghost lifted his head higher and flicked his ears. Kaya held her breath, her hands suddenly cold and sweaty.

Speaking Rain patted Ghost's neck and murmured something Kaya couldn't hear. Ghost relaxed his neck. He shifted his weight and looked around curiously at the gathered people. The stallion's powerful chest and shoulders swelled under his soft, bright silver coat. His black spots shone like the smoothest river stones and his mane and tail flowed silver like waterfalls. He was the most beautiful horse Kaya had ever seen.

Then Speaking Rain swung gracefully from the horse and handed the reins to Kaya.

"Ghost and I are the same in a way," she said to everyone gathered around her, her unseeing eyes turned toward her horse. "We both know what it is to be different—and now we've found each other. So my question now is—what will become of him?

I would never keep a horse near that could hurt our herd, even if—" Her voice caught. "Even if it meant giving up Ghost."

Toe-ta nodded slowly. "It is true that I thought this horse could never be tamed. You have shown me that I was wrong, Daughter. But it is also true that rogue stallions can be a menace to our herd. You are right to ask the question what will become of him. And you will have your answer." He caught the eyes of the other adults, and then Eetsa, Bear Blanket, Jumps Back, and Kautsa followed him into one of the tepees. The flap closed behind them.

Speaking Rain leaned her head against Ghost's neck. Kaya stood just behind her, stroking her back. Neither of them spoke—nor did any of the others sitting nearby. No one got up to start the evening meal. Even Wing Feather and Sparrow sat motionless, their toy arrows stilled in their hands.

"Kaya."

Kaya looked up to see Tall Branch standing in front

of her. A short distance away, Spotted Star was now drinking thirstily from a large bowl of water.

"Kaya," Tall Branch said, "I have falsely accused you of bringing bad luck in the form of the Stick People to our camp." She spoke just as firmly as she had when she was pointing out Kaya's faults. "You have rescued my Spotted Star. Your name is clear. Please accept my apology for bringing shame to you." She held out her hand in a sign of friendship and Kaya clasped it.

"Tall Branch, I accept your apology. Katsee-yow-yow. Though I may not have brought the Stick People to us, I deserved chastisement, since I was careless," Kaya said, trying to match her aunt's clear voice. "I will work hard not to be so again."

Tall Branch gave Kaya a private smile, and Kaya knew her aunt was telling her that they would be friends in the future. Then Tall Branch returned to Spotted Star's side, where she began wiping off the bog mud with a large deerskin.

Speaking Rain still stood by Ghost in silence, and

Kaya stood at her side to wait for the elders' decision. Only once did her sister speak to her. "At least my dream did come true. I did ride him. Ghost and I did find each other—even if it was only for a little while." Her cheeks were flushed and her voice choked. She pressed her forehead to Ghost's. Kaya looked up at the sky to keep the tears that welled in her eyes from falling.

Finally the tepee flap opened and the elders emerged. Kaya stood straight. Speaking Rain clutched Ghost's lead rope. Toe-ta spoke. "You have gone on a daring and dangerous mission, both of you, to rescue Spotted Star. You could have been lost in the bog. And in taming this stallion, you could have been hurt. Speaking Rain, you *were* hurt."

Kaya's heart sank. Toe-ta went on. "But you both believed in this horse—and you believed in yourself, Speaking Rain. Without the work you and Kaya did, Spotted Star would have been lost forever. And without the work you did, this stallion would have been lost forever. But he has learned, through your love, to be gentle again. He may stay with the herd." A smile touched Toe-ta's strong face. "And he may stay with you, Speaking Rain."

Speaking Rain gasped. Kaya squealed and threw her arms around her sister. Speaking Rain hugged Ghost's neck, and they stood that way for a long time, all entwined together. When at last Speaking Rain lifted her head, her face was wet with tears. But she was smiling all over. "I have my horse, Kaya," she said.

Kaya looked at her strong, brave sister. "You and Ghost are finally together—forever. Now you can take care of each other," she said to Speaking Rain. "Just like us."

Inside Kaya's World

In the 1760s, when Kaya was a girl, horses were at the heart of Nez Perce life. Every band or village had its own herd, which could include hundreds of animals. The Nez Perce loved and respected their horses. They relied on them for traveling from place to place with the seasons to hunt, fish, and gather and for journeying to faraway trading partners.

Nez Perce children like Kaya grew up with horses. As infants, they rocked in cradleboards hung from saddle horns. As toddlers, they rode tied to the saddle behind older relatives on mountain trails. By the time they were nine or ten, children were skilled riders, and they knew how to train and care for their horses.

Surprisingly, though, in Kaya's time the Nez Perce people had had horses for only a generation or two. Before then, horses were unknown in the northern plains and mountains. Around 1730, horses brought to the Southwest by the Spanish made their way to Nez Perce country, which lies in parts of what are now Washington, Idaho, and Oregon.

As Kaya learns, however, some Nez Perce believe that long ago, a few special horses came to them from the Pacific Coast. These Ghost Wind Stallions are believed to have been carried aboard a Russian sailing ship and were sent ashore to Nez Perce traders.

Awed by the stallions' strength and beauty, the traders brought them home. When they were bred with Nez Perce mares, their spotted silver coats and strong spirits were passed down to their offspring.

Whether or not the legend is true, horses quickly changed Nez Perce life. On horseback, the Nez Perce could hunt over a much wider territory, even riding out onto the Great Plains in summer to hunt buffalo. The Nez Perce also became skilled at breeding horses. Their fast but sturdy horses, often marked with distinctive spotted coats, became known as Appaloosas—now one of the best-known breeds in America.

It may seem hard to believe that a blind girl like Speaking Rain could ride on her own, but today many visually impaired children and adults take riding lessons to gain muscle strength, balance, and confidence. Some are skilled enough to ride competitively.

Ali Stenis, a Washington teen who has won many awards in dressage events, says she believes that because she is blind, she is actually able to be more in tune with her horse than a sighted rider. Verity Smith, a British rider who is training for the 2016 Paralympics in Brazil, says, "I really believe that horses understand I cannot see. They are very sensitive creatures. They are just magic."

GLOSSARY

In the story, Nez Perce words are spelled so that English readers can pronounce them. Here, you can also see how the words are actually spelled and said by the Nez Perce people.

PHONETIC/ NEZ PERCE	PRONUNCIATION	MEANING
aa-heh/´éehe	*AA-heh*	yes, that's right
Eetsa/Iice	*EET-sah*	mother
katsee-yow-yow/ qe´ci´yew´yew´	*KAHT-see-yow-yow*	thank you
Kautsa/Qáaca´c	*KOUT-sah*	grandmother from mother's side
Kaya´aton´my´	*ky-YAAH-a-ton-my*	she who arranges rocks
Nimíipuu	*nee-MEE-poo*	The People; known today as the Nez Perce
Salish/Sélix	*SAY-leesh*	friends of the Nez Perce who live near them
tawts may-we/ ta´c méeywi	*TAWTS MAY-wee*	good morning
Toe-ta/Toot´a	*TOH-tah*	father

Read more of KAYA'S stories,

available from booksellers and at *americangirl.com*

⊗ *Classics* ⊗

Kaya's classic series, now in two volumes:

Volume 1:
The Journey Begins
Kaya, her sister, and her horse
are captured! If Kaya escapes,
will she ever see Speaking Rain
and Steps High again?

Volume 2:
Smoke on the Wind
As Kaya searches for her
lost sister and beloved horse,
a forest fire threatens all she
holds dear.

⊗ *Journey in Time* ⊗

Travel back in time—and spend a day with Kaya!

The Roar of the Falls

What is it like to live in Kaya's world? Ride bareback, sleep in
a tepee, and help Kaya train a filly—but watch out for bears! Choose
your own path through this multiple-ending story.

⊗ *Mystery* ⊗

Suspense and sleuthing with Kaya!

The Silent Stranger: A Kaya Mystery

Does a strange visitor need help—or will she bring trouble to
Kaya's village?

The Ghost Wind Stallion: A Kaya Mystery

Kaya and Speaking Rain discover a mysterious silver stallion in
the woods. Will he be a blessing or a threat to their people?

A Sneak Peek at

The Silent
Stranger

A Kaya Mystery

Step into another suspenseful
adventure with Kaya!

KAYA SAW THREE horses come over the rise. She recognized her cousins Raven and Fox Tail. Raven was leading a pack horse, which carried someone huddled in a bearskin cloak. Several dogs from the village ran out to meet them, but Tatlo stayed right beside Kaya. Trying to make out who the slumped rider was, Kaya shaded her eyes. Then, as the riders came closer, the bearskin robe slipped back from the stranger's head. Startled, Kaya saw that the stranger wasn't another boy, as she'd thought, but a woman.

Fox Tail jumped off his horse, the halter rope of the pack horse in his hand. Raven helped the woman dismount, for she didn't seem to be able to use her hands. She held them crossed on her chest, as though protecting them. Kaya moved toward the group that had gathered around the stranger.

"I heard the sound of horses," Speaking Rain said. "Who's here?"

"Raven and Fox Tail, and a stranger," Kaya said softly. "A woman."

"A woman?" Speaking Rain asked. "All alone? What does she look like?"

Kaya studied the stranger. The woman was young, with a broad forehead and dark, arched brows, but her head hung and her shoulders were bent. She glanced around as if she didn't know where she was or how she'd come here. "She's pretty," Kaya said, "but she looks very tired. Her hair is in one thick braid instead of two, like ours, and the backs of her hands are tattooed."

"What's she wearing?" Speaking Rain asked.

"Under her bearskin she's got a cape of woven bark with fur at the throat," Kaya said. "She's wearing a necklace of dentalium shells, and abalone ear ornaments, too. She looks like the women who live on the seacoast and come to the Big River to trade."

"*Aa-heh*," Speaking Rain agreed. "But why would someone travel so far in the cold season?"

As Kaya gazed at the stranger, the woman tilted her head a little and glanced Kaya's way. Kaya thought she looked sad, and as if she'd like to ask something. But instead of speaking or making a sign, the woman gazed down again at the ground.

The women and children near Kaya looked curiously at the young woman. Kautsa took charge, as she often did. She strode to where the stranger stood. "Good day!" she said. Then with her hands she threw the words in sign language, *You are welcome here.*

The stranger looked into Kautsa's eyes as if she wanted to respond in some way. After a moment, she shook her head a little and looked at the ground.

"Who is this you've brought to us?" Kautsa asked the boys.

"We don't know who she is," Raven said. "We asked her, but she didn't answer."

"I threw her the words, *Who are your people?*" Fox Tail added. "She didn't answer with signs, either."

"We found her crouched under a hemlock," Raven went on quickly. "Her hands are burned, badly burned. We don't know where she came from or why

she's traveling by herself. But we knew she needed
help, so I got a pack horse for her to ride."

"She let us help her mount," Fox Tail said. "She
wanted to come with us. That's all we know."

"You did well," Kautsa said. "She can't care for
herself with her hands like that, and she shouldn't
travel alone with deep cold coming soon." She
thought a moment before she added, "We need some
warm food for our visitor. It will give her strength."

Kaya knew those words were for her. "I'll get
a bowl of fish soup," she said.

Kaya hurried to her longhouse and came back
with a sheep's-horn bowl of the soup, which she held
out to the stranger. But the woman's gaze suddenly
fell on Tatlo, who sat beside Kaya. The woman's eyes
widened in surprise, and a faint smile came to her
lips. When she bent and held out her hands to him,
Kaya saw that her palms were swollen with blisters.
Tatlo sniffed hard at her hands, all the time looking
up at her face with his amber eyes.

Kaya spooned a piece of salmon from the soup and held it for the woman to eat. But instead, the stranger gingerly lifted the fish from the spoon with the tips of her thumb and forefinger and offered it to Tatlo. He gulped it down, his tail wagging.

"Surely her people don't feed their dogs before they feed themselves," Kautsa whispered.

Kaya offered the spoon a second time. This time the woman drank the soup hungrily, though her gaze lingered on Tatlo as she ate.

The medicine woman, Bear Blanket, made her way to the stranger. Bear Blanket's face was criss-crossed with deep wrinkles and her hair was thin and gray, but she stood straight and held her head high. She gestured toward the stranger's hands and threw her the words, *Are you in pain?*

The stranger lowered her head just a little.

"With her hands like that, she can't speak with signs," Kautsa said to Bear Blanket. "And I don't think she knows our language."

Bear Blanket nodded. *I have medicine that will help your hands,* she signed to the woman. *Come with me.* Motioning for the woman to follow, Bear Blanket led the way to her longhouse.

The soup must have given the stranger strength, for she went with Bear Blanket without hesitation. But she looked back over her shoulder, as if she wanted Tatlo to come, too. Kaya wondered why the woman gave her dog so much attention. To Kaya, he was the best dog ever, but there were many good dogs all around, and the woman hadn't glanced at any of them. Kaya put her hand on Tatlo's head to make sure he stayed by her.

Bear Blanket pulled aside the door flap, and the stranger followed her inside the longhouse. The women and girls began talking about the silent stranger, but Kautsa announced firmly, "Our visitor needs rest now. We'll learn more about her later."

About the Author

First, EMMA CARLSON BERNE thought she was going to be a college professor, so she went to graduate school at Miami University in Ohio. After that, she taught horseback riding to children and adults with disabilities, including those with visual impairment. Then, Emma realized how much she loves writing for young people. Since that time, Emma has authored over four dozen books, including *The Roar of the Falls: My Journey with Kaya* and *Song of the Mockingbird: My Journey with Josefina*. Emma lives in Cincinnati with her three little boys and her husband. She still loves riding horses.